Till I Come Home

Gail Combs Oglesby

Dedication

This book is dedicated to all the women in my family who came before me. I have spent the last forty years learning your stories and this book represents an amalgamation of those historical experiences augmented by my own imagination. In their lives, these women endured heartbreak and sacrifice that can never be truly acknowledged. Yet their gifts of tenacity and strength have flowed down to me across the generations, and for that I am most grateful. I hope I have done justice to your voices and helped you to live on in the hearts and minds of all who read your stories.

The Story Tellers:
We Are the Chosen Ones

*I*n each family there is one who seems called to find the ancestors, to put flesh on their bones and make them live again, to tell the family story and to feel that, somehow, they know and approve. To me, doing genealogy is not a cold gathering of facts but, instead, breathing life into all who have gone before. We are the story tellers of the tribe. All tribes have one. We have been called as it were by our genes.

Those who have gone before crying out to us: Tell our story! So, we do. In finding them, we somehow find ourselves. How many graves have I stood before and cried? I have lost count. How many times have I told the ancestors you have a wonderful family? You would be proud of *us! How many times have I walked up to a grave and felt somehow there was love there for me? I cannot say.*

It goes to pride in what our ancestors were able to accomplish. How they contributed to what we are today. It goes to respecting their hardships and losses, they're never giving in or giving up, their resoluteness to go on and build a life for their family. So, as a scribe called, I tell the story of my family. It is up to that one called in the next generation to answer the call and take their place in the long line of family storytellers.

Excerpt from the poem The Story Tellers attributed

to Della Joann McGinnis Johnson

Contents

Chapter One

The Price We Must Pay

The damp dirt slid slowly off my hand and cascaded onto the casket, a small thumping sound echoing through the air as each clod fell onto the wood below. I try to wipe off my hand on a handkerchief but end up only smearing it across my palm. It fills in each of the lines as if it were a map of my life. I can smell the freshly cut wood of the casket, the name of my son carved into it alongside a small cross. My husband Simon, our four sons, and our daughter then do as I have done.

Then, my brothers James and Stephen, their wives, and their children, and now it is done. My son, Simon William Parkman now lies in the Granary Burying ground next to my father Abel, my mother Rebecca, and my sister Hannah. Nearby lies my other sister Sarah, and our boy Joseph, twin to our son Benjamin who did not survive his first week.

Lieutenant Van Wharton was there to give his condolences on behalf of the 43RD Regiment of Foot led by General William Haviland, a close friend of Simon's father, the late Lord Carrington Parkman. Simon had insisted our son join the ranks of the British fighting against the French and Indians, which I did not protest. Simon looked so dashing in his uniform as he headed off to Montreal. Little did I know I would never see him in it again. His voice still rings in my head, the voice of a man in the face of a child.

"Eliza come we must go now," said my husband quietly in my ear. I hadn't realized I was standing there staring blankly at the casket being lowered into the ground. When my gaze meets his I can see that he is holding back tears as are the boys, only Amelia is openly weeping, her blonde curls bouncing with each sob, her brother John doing his best to console her. So much pain for a girl of not quite nine, her big brother Simon was her favorite to be sure.

Out of the corner of my eye, I see a young woman standing alone next to a casket decorated with the same regiment colors as Simon. She is tall and thin, her long brown hair streaming behind her in the breeze. Lt. Van Wharton excuses himself and joins her as the Deacon says a prayer, his baritone voice carrying across the light breeze. In solitude she stands there, looking not at the casket, but into the distance as if she were trying to pretend that she was somewhere else, anywhere else but here. I want to rush over to her and hold her and tell her it will be fine, but I know in my heart it will not be, it will never be again. Not for her, not for me.

Richard took my arm and guided me across the grass, Simon helping John with Amelia, Benjamin and Nathaniel following quietly behind. I smile a bit as I glance at Richard's profile. He is a handsome boy of fourteen, tall for his age, who looks so much like my father. I wish my mother could see him now, he was still in breeches when she left us. While the sun is warm on my face, the air has a chill and I pull my wrap closer.

"Are you cold, mother?" asks Richard sounding quite concerned. "I could give you my coat?"

"No thank you dearest, I will be fine, we will be home in a few moments," I respond, patting his forearm.

As we walk back along the Boston wharf, I cannot help but think of something my mother used to say, "I will not be gone as long as you remember me, speak well of me, and tell your children of me." She said it was a phrase her mother said to her before she died. It is my duty now to do so for my son who will never have his own children to speak for him. The sounds of the seagulls cawing and the waves lapping at the wharf surround us as we walk slowly, stopping to acknowledge the expressions of sympathy from those we pass along the way.

We are well known in town, and we pass few with whom we are not acquainted in some way. Simon, of course, does business with many. His ships arrive every week with sugar and molasses from his estate in the British West Indies and it is a very profitable enterprise. The molasses is made into rum and distributed widely across the colonies. Ours is a very comfortable life, better than most to be sure, and we enjoy the many benefits that Boston society has to offer.

My great-grandfather, William Tench, was a well-known furniture maker, and he left his business to my grandmother, Alice, when he died as there were no other heirs. My brothers now carry on the business in his name. My grandmother Alice had been born in Boston and she and her husband returned here when my mother was a young girl. Growing up in Boston she felt would provide more opportunity for her children and grandchildren than staying in Plymouth.

She was right, of course; Boston has become the center of colonial life and I would have never met Simon if my grandmother hadn't returned here. Every girl in Boston wanted to marry Simon. He was achingly handsome, well-mannered, and of course from a good family. Although I wasn't the prettiest, he still chose me. My mother said it was because he saw in me a woman who could be more than just something nice to look at. A woman with character, smart and strong.

She said all the women in our family were that way. There were frequent stories of my great-great-grandmother Sarah who had come here as one of the very first colonists. The hardships they endured could not be understated she often said, it is from her we get our strength and our resourcefulness.

It is hard to imagine as I walk through Boston that once this was just a forest, unsullied by English men with only the natives in their villages. Now, it is a melting pot of the world, the French, British, Spanish, Indians and, of course, the negroes which come from the southern continents or the West Indies. Richard helps me up the steps but just as we reach the door the loud song of a bird nearby catches my attention. I turn to look over my shoulder and there, sitting on the high branch of a nearby tree, was a bird. I watch it, crying out for food or perhaps just attention, before it turns and flies away.

"What is it, my dear?" said Simon standing behind me.

"Just a bird, a red-tailed hawk in the tree," I said, smiling to myself as I turned to go inside.

But was it just a bird? For generations our family talked of the hawk and the Indians' belief that it was the spirt of the departed coming to visit those still on this earth. I never told Simon about my family's thoughts about the hawk, I fear he would think it unsophisticated or perhaps just nonsense, but my mother and grandmother believed it. I do too. At least I'd like to think that perhaps that bird was Simon William telling me that he has gone to the heavens, and I need not fear for his soul.

The afternoon is a blur with many callers, they bring cakes and wine, and I am most thankful for Fiona's help. She has been with us for many years now cooking, cleaning, and helping me to dress. She is almost like a friend to me. The children adore her, and you can often hear her singing folk songs from the kitchen, the sweet sounds filling the air. Our dearest Egbert takes care of the horses and the house in general as well as assisting Simon with whatever else he may need, and he has been with him since he was a young man. It is probably time to add another servant because as the boys get older the stables will grow again as will the need for dressing for their many social events. I will speak to Simon.

But now, finally, the house has pulled on its mourning shroud. The deafening silence, the faint tick of the clock, the children's voices finally quiet, the gravity of this day can no longer be escaped. Fiona brings us some wine in front of the fire before excusing herself for the night. Simon puts another log on and pokes it a bit sending up a flurry of embers into the air.

"Do you blame me?" he asks quietly, staring at the flames. He does not have to say more.

"No, of course I do not blame you," I said my eyes softening as he turns to look at me.

"I could not bear it if you did."

He came and sat on the floor at my feet and put his head in my lap as his tears could no longer be held in. I stroked his dark hair as he wept unashamedly for our first-born son, his namesake.

"We did what was right, we must fight for this land if we are to keep it," said Simon.

"Simon William wanted to do his duty," I said quietly.

He nodded, his tears beginning to subside. My tears have been spent and I have no more. My grief now hides away inside me where it will simmer like a low boiling pot, occasionally bubbling to the surface, for the rest of my life. We sit quietly in front of the fire, watching the flames die down till there is nothing left but the red glowing remnants, a metaphor I suppose for our dear son who had burned so brightly in our lives. But there is nothing more to be done, he is gone, I am weary beyond calculation.

"I will check the doors and windows, my dear, and then I will come up," said Simon as he kissed me gently on the cheek.

"Surely Egbert has seen to it?" I said, tilting my head in confusion.

"I am sure he has but I feel the need to be sure, go ahead my dear," he said as he handed me the oil lamp from the table, expertly guiding me to the bottom of the stairs. Slowly making my way up the stairs, I am sure I can hear Simon weeping again. My heart aches for him, for all of us, but none more so than my darling Amelia, the poor child was beside herself with grief today. I quietly open her door and hold up the lamp as I peer into the shadows, relieved to see her curled up in her bed, her blonde curls covering her eyes.

"Mother?" I gasped and grabbed at my throat before my eyes found John emerging from the murky darkness.

"I am sorry, I did not mean to startle you," he said placing his hand on my arm.

"No apology needed my son; I do not know why I was frightened," I said, turning up the lamp to bring more light to the hallway. I could see consternation in his eyes.

"What is it John, is something wrong?" I asked, quietly trying not to wake Amelia as I slowly shut the door.

"I am fine. I heard Amelia's door and came to check on her. I thought you and father were still downstairs."

"I was just looking in on her, but you need not be so watchful my dear, your father and I are here," I said as I stroked his cheek, feeling the coarseness of his beard against my fingers.

He nodded, but I could see there was more.

"I want you to know mother, now that I am, I am...," his voice cracked a bit, "the oldest, I will always do everything in my power to keep you and this family safe."

I pulled him close to me and held him tightly for probably longer than he would have liked, but he did not pull away.

"I know you will John, your father and I think very highly of you and your loyalty to this family is certainly above reproach," I said when I was finally able to speak. He nodded as he took the lamp from me and walked me to my room.

Once inside, I leaned my back against the door, listening to John's footsteps fading away. My heart was pounding so loudly I was sure if there had been another in the room, they would have heard it. My hands shook as I grasped tightly onto the lamp, and I watched the oil splash gently from side to side. I was frightened because his voice, so much like Simon William's, conjured a brief visage of a ghost in the hallway, the son that I had just buried beneath the earth on the hill. It took a few moments for me to regain my composure, but I was finally able to stop my hands from shaking long enough to undo the buttons on my dress. I was already in bed by the time

Simon came in and I was grateful for his presence, and his warmth as I finally closed my eyes … and slept.

Breakfast was a subdued affair, little of the normally boisterous conversation, the sound of glasses tinkling and knives clattering filled the air instead. The one empty chair seemed to glare at me like a silent sentry, keeping watch over the table. I couldn't yet bear to have Egbert remove it.

"Simon, my dear, I think we need to discuss adding another servant to help Egbert," I said, looking up from my toast and jam. In unison, John and Richard looked up at me and then turned to their father.

"Can we, father?" asked John. Simon looked up from his morning copy of the Boston Gazette.

"Yes, I agree with your mother. John, you are coming of age now with Richard not far behind you, and you both will be expected to spend more time with me managing the business, as well as your social engagements," responded Simon smiling a bit at John.

"Father, I was thinking of taking a commission in the British regiment that Simon served in, as soon as I am old enough, of course," said Richard rather quietly.

My heart caught in my throat for a moment, but I did not speak, surely Simon would discourage him.

"Very admirable of you son, but you are too young, perhaps in a couple of years when your studies are complete," said Simon as he reached over and ruffled his hair. I breathed a sigh of relief.

"Besides, you are already serving in the Boston Militia with John and I and soon to include Nathaniel, I think that will suffice."

Richard seemed to accept his father's wishes for now, but I wonder if we shall cross this bridge again in the future. For many years now each colony had maintained its own militia and men above the age of sixteen were required to serve as well as men up to the age of sixty. They trained a few days a year with the goal of providing immediate military support, should it be needed, before British regular troops could arrive.

"Back to the business of finding some additional help," I said clearing my throat. "Fiona, would you have Egbert see me in the sitting room later this morning?" I added as she began clearing the break-fast plates.

"Perhaps you should have John assist you as well, my dear. He needs to learn more about managing this household now that…" his voice trailed off. Now that Simon William is gone, he was going to say, the words unspoken and yet somehow floating on the air as if he had.

"I would be happy to help you mother," said John stopping to kiss me gently on the top of my head as he and Richard made their way out of the dining room.

"May I be excused, mother?" asked Amelia. She had eaten very little, but I could see no point in forcing her to finish, and Benjamin had not said two words all during breakfast.

"Of course, my dear, Nathaniel and Benjamin, you too, go with your sister to the library. I am sure Master Peter will be arriving any moment for your lessons."

"Lessons today," moaned Nathaniel.

"Yes, my darling, lessons today," I responded as I shooed them all off in the direction of the library.

"Amelia, a kiss for your father before you go?" asked Simon hopefully.

"Of course, papa, I always have kisses for you," she said with the hint of a smile before running off with Nathaniel and Benjamin in tow.

Simon loved this little girl more than life itself. He loved the boys too, of course, but Amelia need only smile at him to brighten his whole day. I didn't like my father, I loved him because he was my father, but I did not like him, few people did. I never kissed my father, and he never asked me to.

"Simon, I am worried about her, she has barely eaten in days," I said as Fiona poured us both another cup of tea.

"Time my dearest, she just needs time, she will recover as we all will," he said as he looked at me from the other end of the table. Recover? I did not think I should ever recover from the loss of my child. It is not something you recover from; it is something you simply get through as best you can. The war has dragged on for years but appears to be coming to an end finally, Simon William killed at what they are saying may be the last large battle of this conflict. The

British fighting the French and the Indians taking both sides, betting on who they think might come out the victor. I wonder how many more mothers have cried over sons who will never sit at their table again.

"My apologies Simon, what were you saying." I said, shaking myself out of my own thoughts.

"I have invited Josiah Hutton to dine with us on Saturday, my dear. I hope that will not be an inconvenience."

"No, of course not, you know the captain is always welcome in our home," I said.

Josiah was a fine young man whose father had been a close associate of Lord Parkman's and Simon and the Captain knew each other in London before coming to Boston. He serves in the British Provincial Army leading a militia that guards the harbor.

"He is bringing his sister and aunt as well," added Simon.

"I did not realize he had any relations here in Boston," I said with surprise.

"They arrived just a few weeks ago. They are lodging at the Hawthorn House for now until other accommodations can be arranged."

A dinner party, perhaps this would distract me, help me to turn my thoughts to something other than our loss. It would be good to hear laughter in the house. I must sit down with Fiona today and see what is fresh at the market and plan our meal and, of course, the house will need to be cleaned, much to do.

The week passes quickly, and Saturday has arrived before I know it. Fiona as always has done wonderfully, and the table looks resplendent with its blue and white china against the crisp white linen. The candlelight dances off the beautiful Italian glasses that were my wedding gift from Simon's mother. I work to cut the stems of the flowers Simon has brought and get them arranged into a vase. That was most thoughtful of him, something I should have remembered myself, but did not. My mind still struggles most days to find the order and reliability it had before we lost our son, but it never seems to quite come. Nevertheless, we have prepared as best we can, and I am sure the dinner will be fine.

Benjamin, Nathaniel, and Amelia will eat in the kitchen before our guests arrive. For dinner, just eight of us, Simon, Richard, John, and myself as well as Josiah Hutton, and his sister and aunt whose names I do not yet know. To round out the party, I have also invited Chaplain Browning who serves with Josiah, I do so hate uneven numbers of guests at a dinner party. Richard has been very helpful this week getting the house ready and, as always, Egbert will serve with assistance from his nephew, William, and Fiona's friend, Martha, will lend a hand in the kitchen. We have been most fortunate to have them as I hear tales of woe from many of my friends regarding their help. Egbert is getting on in age, however, so perhaps we shall have to see if his nephew would like to take his place.

The Hutton's, with Chaplain Browning following closely behind arrive right at the appointed hour and I am pleased to see the boys are clean and ready although I did have to wipe a spot of soap from behind John's ear. I smooth the silk of my dress as I stand admiring its embroidered flowers. As I was dressing for tonight, Simon commented that the blue of this dress matches the color of my eyes, and he kissed me on the back of my neck as he helped me with my jewelry. Just this morning, he gave me the most beautiful of pearl necklaces with a large locket suspended from it. Inside there was a small tuft of Simon's hair which he obtained before the coffin was closed. I wrap my fingers around it now, feeling its comfort knowing a small part of him is still nearby.

"Eliza, my dear, you look lovely," smiled Josiah as he crossed the parlor to kiss me gently on each cheek. "It does my heart good to see you looking so well."

"Thank you, Josiah," I said smiling, "you are a welcome sight, as always."

"Mrs. Parkman, may I present my aunt, Mrs. Welles, and my sister, Miss Antoinette Hutton," said Josiah gallantly gesturing toward the two ladies now in front of me. "This is the wife of my dearest friend, Simon Parkman, who you have just met."

"It is so lovely to meet you finally, Josiah has spoken fondly of you and your family for many years," said Mrs. Welles as she took my hand in both of hers, "and I am most sorrowful for the loss of your son Simon," she said, squeezing my hand slightly. I could see the reflection of my own pain in her eyes, and she smiled slightly. She has borne this agony too, it is clear, but a conversation for another day.

"Please, call me Eliza," I replied. "Josiah is like one of the family and we are pleased to welcome you to our home."

She nodded, "You may call me Mary," she replied.

"Miss Hutton, are you finding Boston to your liking?" I said to the young lady.

"Yes, very much so, Mrs. Parkman, it is much larger than I was anticipating" she replied with a large smile. I suddenly realized what a beautiful young girl this was. Her brown hair long and flowing with a hint of red that practically glowed in the candlelight. The dress, a soft shade of green, enhanced her figure while showing off just a hint of her alabaster white shoulders. I was not the only one to notice. John had not taken his eyes off her since she entered the room, and I could see he was standing a bit taller than normal.

"Miss Hutton, my sons, John and Richard," I said as John pushed himself in front of his brother to take Miss Hutton's hand in his. "My pleasure to meet you," he said his voice cracking just a bit as his cheeks turned as red as an apple. Clearly, he was instantly smitten and who could blame him. I am sure Miss Hutton had that effect on most of the young men she met.

"It is lovely to meet you and your family," she said smiling, her eyes shining brightly as they do for the young who have not yet seen pain in their life. John was still holding her hand; I cleared my throat and he let go most reluctantly. I could see this exchange had not escaped the notice of Simon or Josiah, perhaps this is what they planned but their intentions had not been shared with me.

"Shall we go on to dinner?" I said to no one in particular.

"May I escort you, Miss Hutton?" asked John, extending his arm to her. I was sure she could manage the twenty steps to the dining room without assistance, but I appreciated this sudden gallantry on the part of my son who was doing his best to impress the young woman. Simon held my chair, John one for Miss Hutton, and Josiah for his aunt as I heard one chair scraping on the floor and Richard plopping himself down in the chair next to the one his father was standing behind. Well, at least John was showing off his good manners, this one would perhaps need a bit more work.

Simon expertly pulled him back up without embarrassing him, and us, until the women were all seated and settled at the table. But, before Richard could sit down again, John had managed to get to the chair directly across from Miss Hutton, pointing at the chair next to the chaplain as he muttered something under his breath to his younger brother. Richard's glaring look told me he was not pleased but he complied with his brother's request without comment and John was quite pleased with himself.

I chatted pleasantly with Josiah and his aunt while Egbert and William poured the wine, I even acquiesced to Richard having just a bit, perhaps compensation for his displacement from his favorite seat next to his father. Once all the glasses were filled, Josiah rose to his feet, "I would like to make a toast if I may be permitted," he said as he raised his glass looking at Simon.

"Of course!" he responded.

"To our gracious hosts Simon and Eliza Parkman who are my dearest and most loyal friends and to the memory of their son, Simon William Parkman who gave his life in defense of the Crown and its possessions. May his soul rest in peace and may God bring his solace to his friends and family."

It was all I could do to swallow the drink I had taken, and the wine burned as it went down my throat. *"Do not cry, do not cry now,"* I said to myself. Even after all this time, the mention of his name often brought me to tears. I forced a smile, "Thank you Josiah," I said as I reached over and squeezed his hand. "We are so happy to have you and your family here," I said with genuine warmth. It was truly good to have him here and I was enjoying the company.

The evening passed with wonderful food and delightfully interesting conversation and the men did their best not to speak of the war, at least during dinner. Josiah wanted to stay and discuss some business with Simon, so John volunteered to walk Mary and Miss Hutton back to their lodgings as the chaplain was going in the opposite direction. "John, please be sure to take Mrs. Welles arm so that she does not fall in the darkness," I said as they were going out the door. The torches were lit, and it really was not that dark outside, but I knew if I had not mentioned it John would be holding on to Miss Hutton without a thought for Mary's safety.

"Thank you, Eliza, for a wonderful evening, perhaps we could do tea later this week?" said Mary before she departed.

"I would like that very much," I replied, as Egbert closed the door behind them. "Wonderfully done Egbert. Would you let Fiona know I am not going up just yet. I want to join Simon and Josiah in the library for a few moments."

"Thank you, ma'am, it was my pleasure, and I will most certainly let Fiona know. I am sure she will appreciate more time in the kitchen," Egbert responded in that always soothing voice of his. I have never heard him raise it in anger or even excitement. He is always the same, like the constant drip of the faucet, the tone of which never changes.

Simon and Josiah were deep in discussion, their heads bent towards each other and away from the door, and I hesitated a moment in the doorway of the library.

"Eliza dear is everything good?" said Simon and Josiah rising simultaneously from their chairs.

I nodded, "Yes, Egbert has it well in hand as always. I wanted to talk with Josiah for a few moments if I may."

"Eliza, here please take my chair," he said as Simon pulled up another chair from the other side of the room for him.

It took me a moment to collect my thoughts and I was grateful for the small glass of apple brandy Simon had fetched for me. The men looked at me expectantly but patiently and I took another small sip before I asked the question that had been burning in my mind.

"Josiah, I know much time has passed, but do you know anything more than we have been told about how Simon William died?" I said quietly. Simon leaned back in his chair and sighed.

"Eliza, are you sure you want to hear about this? Nothing I say will bring Simon William back to you," said Josiah looking back and forth from me to Simon perhaps trying to gage his feelings on the matter.

"It is fine, if she wishes to know, it is her right as his mother," said Simon with a resigned air. "If you do not tell her now, she will simply ask again."

He was right of course, I would ask again, and again if need be until I understood what happened to my son. Josiah pulled his chair closer to mine and took my hand in his.

"Eliza, please stop me if you feel at any moment that this is more than you wish to know," said Josiah with a more serious tone than I had ever heard from him.

I nodded as Simon came and stood behind me, his hand resting on my shoulder. Grateful for his presence I laid my hand on his and kept it there should I need his reassurance. Some may not want to know, some may simply accept what has happened and move on, but not me. I had to know, no, I desperately needed to know, exactly what happened the day my son died.

"As you know, General Wolfe was leading the charge that day against the French forces led by

Montcalm. The General decided to scale the cliffs leading up to Quebec City and attack the French from a direction they would not anticipate. His plan worked, and he and his men were able to fight the French on the plains of the farm near which they were camped. You know, of course, that General Wolfe died during the battle?" asked Josiah clearing his throat.

"Yes, I understand a terrible loss. I understand."

"When General Wolfe was hit by musket fire, Simon was behind him in his role as the General's aide. He immediately dropped his own weapon and he and another soldier grabbed the General and tried to get him on his feet to take him back away from the line of fire. Before they could turn and retreat, the General, and the other soldier were hit again with volleys of musket fire, killing them both. Simon picked up his fallen musket and began advancing again, now with many of the soldiers following his lead. They moved toward the enemies' right flank and there Simon and the men spotted Montcalm leading the French attack. They fired, killing him, but in the process Simon and several others were mortally wounded."

My fingers folded around the edge of Simon's hand ... I was afraid to ask. "Did he suffer, tell me true," I said, looking Josiah squarely in the eye.

"No Eliza, he did not suffer, and his bravery helped us to win the battle and most likely the war," he said softly.

He didn't suffer ... I could feel the iron bonds that had encased my chest breaking free and breath filling my lungs for the first time in these many, many months. I sat quietly for a moment, no one spoke.

"Thank you, Josiah, truly your words have comforted me," I said as I rose from the chair. "Now if you will both pardon me, I will take my leave."

Simon kissed me and then rang for Egbert who escorted me up the stairs where Fiona was waiting to help me undress. She could tell I didn't want to talk, and she went about her work quietly, helping me out of my dress and taking down my hair. As she brushed my long locks, I could feel myself relax, my shoulders easing down to a more normal state.

It is a sad truth that the people of the world fight over land, or power, and perceived violations of their rights. Sometimes I just wonder if men fight because it is simply their nature, like the stallions in the field, thrashing at each other with their hoofs. The British are desperately afraid of the French and will do anything to keep them from taking more of this land. Once upon a time, it was the French beating back the Dutch and the Colonists fighting the natives.

In my soul, I know this has been this way since the start of civilization. There is so much in this world, so much land, so much prosperity, is it necessary to fight with each other over the same spit of land? Perhaps it will end someday, and men will find a more peaceful way to resolve their differences. But for now, the lives of young men are the price that must be paid.

Chapter Two

Children No More

Miss Hutton, Antoinette, and her Aunt Mary have become regular visitors at the house over the last two years and as predicted, John and Antoinette are very much in love. Both Simon and Josiah thought them too young to marry quickly and so they have had a protracted engagement, but the time is drawing close. Simon has always thought of Josiah as a brother and now our families will be united for life. Antoinette is an accomplished and intelligent young woman, there is substance beneath that beautiful face and I'm sure she will make a wonderful wife for John. I've never seen him so happy, and it truly warms my heart. He spends more and more of his time with Simon at the docks, managing shipments and coordinating deliveries. He has quite a head for business and Simon is most pleased with his efforts.

The war is finally over, and a treaty was signed in Paris last year. British soldiers fill the streets of Boston and there have been several balls and celebrations to honor their victory. It saddens me that Simon William is not here to share in the accolades, but his heroism is spoken of often and my pain is eased by my pride in him. Richard seems to have lost the desire to have a military career, at least for now, and John is encouraging him to take more of an interest in their father's business. I'm not sure that business is going to satisfy him, however, as he has more than a bit of restlessness which drives him from one thing to the next as if he were a butterfly flitting from bloom to bloom.

"Mother," said Amelia, breaking my silent contemplations.

"Yes, my dear?"

"Master Peter would like to speak with you if you have a moment," she said very formally, before turning to run back upstairs giggling, almost running over him in the process.

"Good morning, ma'am" said Peter laughingly as he expertly side-stepped her to avoid a crash.

"Good morning, Peter," I said with a smile. "Please do sit down," I said as I motioned to the chair across from me. "She is quite a handful, isn't she?"

"She is a lovely young lady ma'am and a joy to have in class, she is very bright and works very hard, she and boys too," he said still smiling, "In fact, that's why I am here."

"Go on."

"I think that both Benjamin and Nathaniel would benefit from attending the new academy being opened by my former teacher, Mr. Burton. There, they would have access to a wider variety of teachers in expertise I do not have like French, for example," he explained.

"French? Why would the children need to learn French given that we have just won the war against them and sent them north." I replied, clearly perplexed at his suggestion.

"The French may have lost the war, but they will not be leaving the colonies entirely, and they are still a force in the world as we know it. Also,

French is widely spoken in New France. Many there do not speak English, and if you can speak French you can easily learn other languages that share the same roots."

"I see," I said thoughtfully, "and what of Amelia?"

"There are other young girls her age from prominent families in Boston who will be attending so I believe. If you are willing, she could join the boys, although not in the same classes, of course."

"I must speak to my husband as this is a decision we both must make but I think there is merit in your proposal, so let us see what he has to say."

"Thank you, ma'am, I appreciate your consideration," he replied, rising from his chair.

"Peter, if we decided to put the children in the academy, where would you go? You have been with us for many years now and I would not want to see you without an employer."

"That is most kind of you, Mrs. Parkman. I have decided to return to England," he said with a hint of sadness. "My parents are both aged, and they need someone to help care for them. Marie, my only sibling, died last year and so now they have no one."

"That is very admirable of you, Peter. I am sure your parents will be grateful to have your presence once again. I will speak with Simon this evening."

Peter's departure would be a sadness, especially for the children, but I think perhaps he is right, it may be good for them to have broader horizons than those that he can offer. Benjamin continues to be melancholy and so perhaps this is just the change he needs. Nathaniel and Amelia are as easy-going as the breeze, and I am sure this would be of no consequence to them other than their sadness over Master Peter.

Simon readily agreed and in no time the music of the house changed with no sounds of laughing children or footsteps on the stairs. It saddens me to think that my children will soon be children no more. But the days are filled with teas and preparations for the wedding which seem to dominate more and more of the calendar. It is good for the children to be able to focus on happier times and I have seen a change in Amelia most decidedly and her demeanor seems to have improved finally.

After dinner I joined Simon in the library. It was obvious something is troubling him, having barely spoken to me or the children all evening. "My dearest, may I sit with you?" I asked, peeking around the door frame. Simon was puffing away on his pipe but quickly rose to his feet, "Of course Eliza, I am glad you came," he said as he kissed me on the cheek before pulling up a chair for me at his desk.

"I can see something is on your mind."

He smiled at me, that shy smile he has when he has been caught doing something he knows I will not approve of. It is a boyish smile, and it always makes my heart beat a bit faster.

"Oh, my dear, I should know by now that very little escapes your attention," he said softly as he laid his pipe on the desk.

"Well, very little in this family at least, beyond that I cannot say," I said confidently. "What is it?"

Simon leaned back in his chair and stared at the ceiling for a moment. I could tell by his hesitation that whatever was on his mind was not going to be welcome. "News has begun to filter to me from England regarding an edict which is about to be published by the King," he said with a serious tone. George III had been King for the last three years or so and his efforts to push back the French had been a great success so I couldn't imagine what could possibly be of such concern to Simon now.

"Go on," I said hesitantly.

"He is concerned about the cost of the ongoing defense of the colonies, this war with France having been a drain on England's coffers. So, he intends to prohibit all settlement west of the Appalachian Mountains unless he can obtain guarantees of security from the Indian nations."

"Surely this does not affect us," I said with a quizzical air.

"Directly, no it does not, but I do not believe this news will be received well by the leadership of the colonies. They believe in their own right to decide how to manage the lands to the west."

"Well, that may be but if the King prohibits it, what recourse do they have?"

"That, my dear, remains to be seen," said Simon with a tone both foreboding and questioning.

We spoke of it no more, and while there was grumbling from time to time at dinner parties and balls, nothing seemed to come of it. It was clear, however, that the King was stationing more and more troops in the colonies to protect what had been so hard won against the French. Josiah was now in charge of the King's soldiers stationed in Boston and his command center was near Simon's office on the wharf. One cannot walk for more than a few minutes through town without encountering a soldier or two.

John and Antoinette are to be married in just two weeks' time and there is to be a party in their honor next week. Simon could not be happier, nor could I, as I can clearly see how very much they are in love. Not all marriages are for love, but it certainly makes them more tolerable when they are. My mother never pressured me to marry for station or advantage for which I was most grateful although I managed to do both. My grandmother, Alice, had told her that her love for my grandfather, Abraham, was one of the great joys of her life.

Oddly, I cannot say if my mother felt the same way about my father. I never heard them quarrel or be cross with each other but that is not the same as love. When my father died, my mother wept most vigorously and I was sure that her sorrow was genuine, but still. In my presence, I never saw a tender moment between them. Not a touch of her hand on his shoulder or his kiss on her cheek. I brushed the thought from my mind and focused instead on the needlework in my hands. I must get this dress completed for Amelia; it will be her first real social event and I want it to be perfect. My eyes tire quickly and for a moment I lean back in my chair and close my eyes and before I know it, my mind fills with a swirl of memories from the past.

The day Amelia was born was dark and overcast and the wind and rain blew so hard against the house that it sounded like someone was throwing pebbles at the windows. Some gusts were so strong, the whole house seemed to shudder and moan like old women do when they rise from a chair. My birthing was moving quickly, and I was worried that Simon would not make it in time. Unlike most men who left the job of birthing to the women, he had been with me for the births of all our children, and I knew he would be disappointed were he not here for this one.

Truly I need not have worried, he arrived just in time, soaked to the skin. Holding tightly onto my hand and doing his best to dry himself with the other hand, it was only a moment or two more before she was born.

"It is a girl," said Mrs. Jensen, the mid-wife, as she handed this little bundle to Simon.

I could see the tears welling up in his eyes as he pulled back the blanket from her face to get a better look.

"She is beautiful, my dearest, just like her mother," he said, smiling from ear to ear as he handed her to me.

He was right, she was perfect in every way, her little pink mouth turned up like a little bow, her fat cheeks red from my efforts. She even had just a tiny bit of hair, much lighter though than the boys were born with. We had already decided that if the child were a girl we would name her after our mothers. Amelia, Simon's mother, died giving birth to his younger brother, David, who passed when he was only three. My mother, Rachel, had died just over a year ago and sadly would never meet her granddaughter.

Amelia Rachel Parkman, what a fine name I thought as I opened my eyes and wiped away a small tear that had leaked out of my eye and onto my face. How could it be that my tiny babe is now a beautiful young girl of nearly twelve. There are no more children in our home and that knowledge comes with a great sadness, but there will be grandchildren soon enough and the thought makes me smile.

Unbeknownst to John and Antoinette, we have purchased from the Widow Thomas a small house for them just around the corner from us. She can no longer live alone and has gone to live with her daughter in Virginia. The home is a modest one, but it will be perfect for them for a few years at least, and it will be nice to have them nearby. Richard has been calling on a young lady for a few months, but I hear little of it, so I do not think it is of much importance.

He has an air of agitation about him, this one, and I do not think we will hold him in Boston much longer. He has a great desire to see more of the world and Simon has talked with him about going to the plantation in the West Indies to help with operations there. I hate the thought of him being so far away, but Simon is getting of an age where the trips to visit his holdings there take much more of a toll on him than they did when he was a virile young man.

Women do their best to make peace with growing old in whatever form it takes. But men simply pretend it is not happening until their bodies finally begin to betray them, often at the most inconvenient times. I am sure Richard's future will be the topic of much conversation, but first, this dress and the wedding.

It is a beautiful day, and everyone is resplendent in their finest suits and dresses. Antoinette is breathtaking and even John, who I have not seen cry since he was in breeches, could not contain his emotions. We sit in our box pew in the front, not our regular spot a few rows back. The church is full of families we have known these many years and soldiers from Josiah's regiment. Their red coats with their polished brass buttons are a bright contrast against the stark white wood. The white benches are decorated with finely arranged greenery and just a hint of a pale pink flower, nearly the shade of the blush on Amelia's cheeks. I cannot help but notice many of the soldiers are looking at her most intently. She is too young, on this I will be firm, not my youngest, not yet.

A small reception at the home now occupied by Mary Welles is a delight, but it is still hard to think of John as a man with a wife. She glows when she looks at him, Antoinette, and all can see that this is a love match indeed. When Simon announced the gift of their new home the entire party applauded and yelled out their "well done" raising their glasses to the good health of the newly-married couple. It was a wonderful day and a resplendent celebration, but it is unsettling as I put out the light to know that John will no longer be sleeping down the hall. Tonight, he sleeps a few blocks away with his wife, and from now on he belongs more to her than to me.

Does a child ever really belong to their parents? I suppose not, not in the way a slave belongs to a slave owner, of course, but there is an expectation, I believe, that one's child has an obligation to their parents. They should be of help or comfort when needed, support their role in the community, and certainly assist in raising their siblings. John has been all of that and more and his presence will be missed.

But soon other issues will become more pressing than just my melancholy regarding my oldest son's absence.

"Well, it is about damn time," said Simon, unexpectedly slapping his copy of the Boston Gazette onto the breakfast table. I look up from my plate, startled by his sudden outburst and his language only to catch Richard snickering under his breath at his father's indiscretion.

"I am sorry, my dear," he added before I could even chastise him for his vulgarity.

I nodded my acceptance; grateful that the younger children had already gone to school.

"Parliament has finally decided to crack down on these Dutch and French smugglers bringing rum to the colonies."

"That is wonderful news, father, now perhaps we will get a fair deal in the market and expand our business," replied Richard as he buttered yet another biscuit.

Simon looked up at me and tilted his head to the side, the way he does when he is wondering if I will object to what he says next. It is a good thing he is not much of a card player; he is very easy to read, at least for me.

"Richard, your mother and I have not discussed this at any length, but I think it might be appropriate timing for you to go and visit our estates in Barbados to ensure that things are running smoothly and to determine if we can ramp up additional production."

I stared back at him, my face a blank canvas on which I had not yet determined what would be written. To say we had not discussed it at length was to say that it had not been mentioned more than in passing and that was some time ago. Despite that, I knew Simon was right and that Richard wanted to go, no … needed to go would be more accurate. Richard was watching me intently but knew enough to keep my own composure as he waited expectantly.

"I agree with…" I couldn't even finish my sentence before Richard was up out of his chair nearly dancing around the table and laughter rose from my chest and out of me that I hadn't heard in some time.

Despite my trepidation in having him so far away, it did my soul good to see him so happy. The arrangements were made quickly, and Richard was to set sail in just four days' time. We gathered over dinner the next night knowing it would be many months before we would do so again. It was a bittersweet gathering made even more poignant by John's announcement that Antoinette is with child. I am going to be a grandmother and the thought brings me great comfort.

"You will write to me at least once per week," I said to Richard as I tucked his scarf in around his jacket collar more tightly.

"Yes, of course mother, I will write to you each week," he said as he kissed me on each cheek.

I held tightly onto his shoulders which seemed broader than I remembered. My son, this man, off half a world away, I could only pray that God would keep him safe. Amelia hugged him tightly and he whispered something in her ear that made the impending tears turn to smiles. Nathaniel and Benjamin shook hands with Richard as if they were oh so grown up. Simon, however, did not hesitate to embrace him, and I could see him beaming with pride as his son carried his bag up the gangway and onto the ship.

We stayed in the harbor until the lines were cast and the ship began to drift out of the harbor. Richard stood at the bow and waved to us for as long as he could before the ship slipped from our sight. As we walked back toward the house, I could see a change happening around us. Voices were more animated, and it seemed as if more and more people were filling the streets, the crowds all moving in the direction of Market Square.

"Simon, what is happening?" I asked, tightening my grip on his arm while pulling Amelia closer to me.

Simon was now furiously looking in every direction trying to gauge our circumstances.

"I am not sure, my dear, but I think it would be best if you went home," he said.

"Soldier!" Simon called out to a passing young man in uniform. "Are you with Captain Hutton's command?" he demanded.

"I am sir," came the breathless reply.

"Please, I am Simon Parkman, and this is my wife, our children and my son John and his wife who is Captain Hutton's niece. Could you escort my family to our home?"

"Of course, sir, I am sure the captain would approve."

"John, come with me. Antoinette, please go with Eliza and the children. Benjamin, you get Egbert and lock up the house as soon as you are all safely inside," yelled Simon over his shoulder as he hurried off with John in the direction of the square.

"I am coming too, father," Benjamin replied, sprinting after Simon who turned to grab him by the shoulders.

"No son, I need you to stay with your mother, now do as I say," he said almost angrily before turning once again to join the sea of men.

"Do you have any idea what is happening?" I asked the soldier as we hurried through the streets.

"I do not know for certain Ma'am, but there was talk at the regimental headquarters this morning that news had come from England regarding a new tax. Beyond that I do not know what the trouble might be."

I could hear shouting from the square as we drew closer to our home and the stream of men filling the streets now had choked all wagon traffic to a halt. Women and children stood on every stoop and the consternation was visible on their faces as we hurried past the rows of fine homes. On the street which ran parallel to our own, I saw some men carrying an effigy on a wooden pole which they had set on fire, but I could not tell who it was intended to represent. Once inside, Benjamin quickly did as his father had asked, the shutters were closed and the doors bolted in a matter of moments. He then took a musket for himself from the closet in Simon's study and he handed another to Egbert and one to Nathaniel.

"Mother, please take Amelia, Aunt Nettie, and Fiona and go upstairs," said Benjamin quietly.

Nathaniel is just a boy, I said to myself, staring at him holding this rifle. I hesitated, my mind whirling, as I could feel the fear rising in me.

"Mrs. Parkman, we should go upstairs as Benjamin says," said Antoinette, taking my elbow and guiding me toward the stairs.

Of course, she was right, and her with child.

"Egbert you watch the back door, Nathaniel, I want you to watch the windows on the east side of the house, I will take the front door," I could hear Benjamin saying as I closed and bolted the bedroom door. Fiona had the presence of mind to grab some water, wine, and biscuits and we made a bit of a picnic on the floor, doing our best to distract each other, especially Amelia, who had grown very quiet. I could still hear voices on the street, men shouting and then, the sound of breaking glass and a loud thud.

Fiona raced to the door and peeked out to find Benjamin in the hallway picking up a large rock.

"Go back inside Fiona," he said in a voice barely above a whisper as he picked it up and pushed the shards of glass to the side with his foot.

"I will clean that up, Master Benjamin," she said as she knelt carefully picking up the pieces and putting them in her apron.

"Later, Fiona, now please go back in the bedroom," he said as he helped her up from the floor. I could see the bits of blood on her apron as she shut the door behind her.

"Fiona, what is it? Are you hurt?"

"No ma'am, it is just a bit of broken glass, someone … someone…," she faltered, either unable to find the right word or unable to say it.

"Fiona, speak what is it," I said, my voice expressing more fear than I would have liked in front of Amelia.

"A rock, someone threw a rock through the window," she said finally.

Amelia looked at me with a fear in her eyes I had not seen since Simon William died. A fear only a young girl can feel, one so lacking in control over their own life and destiny.

I pulled her close to me, "Do not worry, my darling, your father and brothers will protect us," I said as I kissed her on the top of her head. "Fiona, come here to the basin, let us get those cuts washed up."

The sun had nearly set by the time there was a knock on the door.

"Mrs. Parkman, it is safe to come out," said Egbert, his reassuring voice a most welcome sound.

I breathed a sigh of relief as Fiona helped me up from the floor and I raced downstairs with Amelia and Fiona following quickly behind to find Simon and the boys in the study.

"Fiona, can you get some meat, cheese, and bread and bring it to the study? Amelia can you also ask Egbert to bring a cask of ale from the larder, these men look tired and hungry?"

"What is happening?" I asked Simon as I looked from face to face.

"Just some rabble-rousers upset about some news from Parliament," replied Simon wiping the beads of sweat off his brow.

"It is nothing for you to be concerned about, mother," said John in a tone that was more condescending than I felt was appropriate.

"Someone threw a rock through the window of my home so if it is a matter that impacts my family I will decide how, and when, I will be concerned," I snapped angrily.

I could see John was taken aback. I seldom spoke to the boys in this manner, but my anxiousness had built up over the course of the afternoon and, unfortunately, he was on the receiving end of my emotion. I winced seeing how my words had wounded my eldest son.

"John, your mother is right, this is a matter that impacts us all and as such she has every right to be concerned," said Simon as he rose wearily from his chair to wrap his arms around me.

I am not sure why, but I began to cry and soon I could feel John and Benjamin, each with a hand on my shoulder.

"I am sorry mother," said John, clearly distressed by my tears. I turned and wrapped my arms around him.

"I am the one who should be sorry, my son. I know your words were meant as a kindness and truly I am apologetic for having lost my temper with you," I said as I kissed him on the cheek.

"Eliza, sit down. Nathaniel, fetch your mother a brandy please," said Simon as he sat down next to me, and at last offered an explanation.

"Word arrived today that Parliament has passed something called the Stamp Act. To raise monies for the continuing defense of the colonies, there will soon be a tax on stamps required for documents, licenses, bonds, and the like, official papers that are required to do business. Needless to say, that news was met with a great deal of angst from the local citizenry who do not feel that Parliament has the right to tax us as citizens of the Colonies. The men gathered in Market Square to express their discontent by looting and burning and threatening the Governor and the Tory leaders of the community."

"The home of Andrew Oliver, the Massachusetts stamp distributor, was mobbed and vandalized. He had no choice but to resign," added John, shaking his head in disbelief.

"I do not understand, we are all citizens of Britain and loyal to the crown, how could they possibly object to the government's efforts to raise monies for our defense?

"It is not that simple, my dear, you know the Tories and Whigs have long been at odds with each other about how much, or how little, England should interfere with government in the colonies," replied Simon.

Benjamin was quietly gazing out the window to the street which was still filled with throngs of people and horses.

"Many say it is taxation without representation as we have no direct representatives from the Colonies in Parliament, so they have no right to levy these illegal taxes," he said as he turned to look at his father and brother.

"That is nonsense, you are a child you know nothing of this," spat John as he waved a dismissive hand.

"I am not a child!" he screamed back at John, his face turning a crimson shade of red. "I read, I listen, and it is not nonsense brother, it is what many think is fair and right, that if we are truly British subjects then we should have a say in what happens in British government. If not, then perhaps we should govern ourselves instead."

His words hung in the air as if they were perched on the edge of a guillotine about to crash down on us at any moment and both Simon and John physically recoiled, as if to avoid the blade.

"Benjamin, that is enough," said Simon rising to his feet, his fist clenched against his thigh as if he had intended to strike him but thought better of it.

Without another word, he turned and ran up the stairs to his room and slammed the door behind him.

"Father, that is treason, you need to speak to him now," said John as he ran his fingers through his dusty mop of hair.

"That is enough from you as well, and do not ever speak that word again about anyone in this family, do you hear me?" said Simon as he angrily pointed his finger at John just inches from his face.

He nodded his understanding at his father, "Good night, mother," he said before he quickly left the house, disappearing into the night.

I sat motionless in my chair. I could not even begin to comprehend what I had just witnessed. Never in all my days have I ever heard Benjamin speak with such emotion on issues of politics only to have his father and brother respond in kind.

"Simon, why would someone throw a rock through our window?"

"Because those that are angry with Parliament and the crown want to harass those that they perceive to be loyal to King and country."

"Will they continue to attack us?"

"People have long been quick in this town to voice their discontent but as it always does it will blow over and the citizenry will come to its senses, Benjamin too," he replied before downing his brandy in one gulp before slamming his glass on the desk.

Chapter Three

The Twists and Turns of Life

B ut he was wrong, so very wrong. Since that night some three years ago nothing has been the same, and all the talk in town is driven by the same idea of resistance to acts of Parliament and talk of self-governing. The Sons of Liberty they call themselves, Simon calls them the Sons of Despotism, a group of prominent statesmen in the colonies who have banded together to argue against Parliament's ability to tax the colonies without their consent. The Stamp Act was repealed not long after it was instituted but that was not the end of it, truly it was the beginning of the end, we just did not realize it yet.

The Declaration Act, passed by Parliament over a year ago, asserted the rights of the English government to make laws binding to the colonies in any way they chose. Now, it is the Townshend Act, a tax on glass, lead, paper and, worst of all, tea. The taxes have little impact on us truly, as our coffers are full, but now everyone is impacted by this new attempt by the British government to squeeze more and more from the colonies. Simon is concerned about the increasingly frequent boycotts of products from Britain, which what we import certainly is, but the business is still doing well given that citizens have few other choices with the blockades on Dutch and French goods being smuggled in.

Benjamin spends his days at the warehouse with Nathaniel now away at law school at William and Mary, but he spends every visit home railing against the injustice of English rule with support from Benjamin. Simon and John are on one side of the table and they on the other, my house has become a home divided. And we are not the only ones. Simon is loyal to the crown as he always will be, the same with John and his allegiance to the role of the British military in the colonies, as you would expect. After all, the now Major Hutton is uncle to his children,

Simon William who we lovingly call Willie and his little sister, Elizabeth.

Richard, still in Barbados, does not speak about this issue in his correspondence, but Simon is asking him to return home so we will soon know his opinion on the matter. Either way, one or more of my children will be at odds with the other. It is a sad situation indeed and one which I do not see a clear path out of. No one really asks me what I think, and I am not sure I know myself. I am of this land. My grandmother was born here, and my mother and now my grand-children. Are we English? Yes, I suppose we are, but perhaps we are also of our own keeping, our own mind. But for now, at least, I hold those thoughts only in the quiet corners of my mind, sharing them with no one lest it add to the tension that is already at times more than I can bear.

"Richard will be here at the end of the week," said Simon looking up at me from the letter in his lap, peering over his recently acquired spectacles.

I thought they made him look distinguished, even more handsome as the gray begins to take over more and more of his hair.

"That is wonderful news, I am most anxious to see him," I responded with a smile.

As he had promised, he has written dutifully these past years, nearly every week. Only during a period of sickness last winter did we not hear from him directly for nearly a month. I think he would be very happy to stay on in Barbados, but Simon wants him home for reasons I do not fully know, but with which I have no quarrel. The time passes quickly as Fiona and I work to prepare his old room and clean the house. It is hard to believe he has been gone for so long, what I thought would be only a few months has now become many years, and the boy that left is now a man.

"The ship is arriving, Mrs. Parkman," said Egbert interrupting my mending. My heart skips a beat in anticipation.

"Wonderful," I reply.

"I have the carriage waiting."

Simon and the boys are already at the wharf, so it was just Amelia and I in the carriage, oh and Sargent Wood, of course. For the last year private citizens have been asked to quarter the ever-increasing number of soldiers in town, providing them with a place to sleep and provisions. Of course, we were happy to oblige, and Major Hutton sent us Sargent Wood, and Captain Meeden is with John, Antoinette, and the children. Whenever we travel without Simon or one of the boys, the Sargent is with us. It is a comfort really and he is most polite and helpful.

I can see Simon, John, and Benjamin waiting on the wharf. It is unfortunate that Nathaniel could not be here, but he will arrive tomorrow. As Simon helps me out of the carriage, I look up and see Richard standing at the railing and I wave at him excitedly, but he does not see me. He is busy chatting with a woman standing next to him as he points to various buildings along the wharf. I wave again.

"Richard," I call out over the hustle and bustle of the wharf.

Finally, his head turns in my direction, and he smiles as he waves, again speaking to the woman next to him. As she turns slightly to get a better view, I can see that she is with child as she puts her arm through Richard's and smiles up at him. I look at Simon, he is scowling and shaking his head, clearly whatever this situation with Richard is, it was apparently not known to him.

Richard helps the woman down the gangplank as she gently picks her way between the slats, holding on to her protruding belly as if it would somehow slip away from her were she not careful. Even from this distance you can see that she is a beauty, her ink black hair piled on top of her head and spilling down onto her back in a cascade of curls. She is a delicate creature with a small frame and feminine features, her skin the color of tea with just a drop of milk, and the weight of the child she is carrying looks as if it will overwhelm her at any moment. Impeccably dressed, she smiles again at Richard, and I can see at once that they are very much in love.

"Mother," his voice finally rings out as he waves at the bottom of the gangplank and its familiar sound is a joy to hear.

In just a moment, he is in my arms and holding him close to me melts my heart. The woman stands by shyly as Richard makes the rounds of handshakes and embraces but now, we all wait expectantly.

He clears his throat, "Mother, father, meet my wife, Susannah Thorne Parkman. Her father, Sir Robert Thorne, is the Adjunct General of Barbados," he said as he took her elbow and expertly guided her until she was standing right in front of me.

I drew in my breath and held it for a moment trying to steady myself. *Not a word,* I thought to myself. How could he have not told his family that he was married, and that she was with child! *Breathe, just take a deep breath, what is done is done,* I thought as I exhaled slowly.

"My dearest Susannah, it is a pleasure to meet you, I only wish we had known about your arrival sooner so that we would have been more prepared," I said as I took her hand in mine.

"I am sorry for that Mrs. Parkman. I wanted Richard to write you about this … about us," she said with a slight smile. "But he thought it best to tell you in person," she said glancing over at him.

"She is entirely right mother. I wanted to surprise you, and the family," he said grinning from ear to ear.

"Well, you have certainly done that."

Simon and Egbert set about gathering their belongings as I made the rest of the introductions. Amelia seemed as smitten with Susannah as her brother and immediately took control of getting her into the carriage with her and Antoinette.

"Richard, you can ride with your mother and I," said Simon in a slightly gruff tone as he steered him toward the second carriage that was now waiting.

"John and Benjamin will come along with the trunks shortly.

I could see Richard had a look of sheer panic on his face as it was clear his father meant to have words with him out of the earshot of his new bride. Reluctantly, he climbed aboard and sat with his back to Sargent Wood who was kind enough to drive for us.

"Sargent, drive the long way back to the house if you would please," said Simon as he settled in next to me.

There was no escaping now, he knew he was trapped.

"It is wonderful to see you both, mother you look as though you have not aged a day since I left," said Richard forcing a smile. "Father, the glasses make you look most handsome, mother had mentioned to me that you were now wearing them."

Stone-faced, Simon and I looked at him, saying nothing, only the clip-clop of the horse hooves providing the backdrop for our ride.

"So, your mother mentions to you that I now wear spectacles, but you do not think to mention that you have married, and that the woman is with child?" said Simon finally.

"That woman is my wife," he retorted.

"Apparently," responded Simon rather sarcastically.

"I'm sorry I should have written but our marriage was rather … sudden, and I truly felt it was best to wait and tell you in person. I am not a child; I am quite capable of making my own decisions. I hoped you would be happy for me,"

"Were you forced to marry her?" said Simon staring directly at Richard.

"Of course not, father, surely you do not think so little of me that you would believe I would take this woman's honor and marry her only out of duty," he spat back at Simon.

"No one has said such a thing, son, but you must understand that this has come as quite a shock to us," I replied as I reached out and took his hand.

He squeezed it in his, much like he did that day he held my hand as we walked home after Simon William's burial.

'I love Susannah, with all my heart, and I hope you will learn to love her too. She is my wife, and she is having my child," he said firmly.

"And what of this woman's … your wife's family, they approve of this marriage?"

"Yes father, they approve most heartily although I think her mother, Mrs. Thorne, was not pleased that we left the island."

"Her mother is also British?" I asked, the question I wanted to ask masked behind this one instead. Susannah was a beautiful woman indeed but a white woman, I did not think so.

"I know what you are hinting at mother, you need not be so coy," said Richard as I could feel myself blushing.

"Susannah's grandmother was a mulatto, her family having been brought to the islands from Africa some eighty years ago, she married a Spaniard. Her mother married Sir Robert and she bore him two boys and three girls."

I looked at Simon and I could see the concern in his eyes.

"Son, as you say, you are not a child. You are a grown man and you have done admirably helping to manage our business in the islands. Cleary you are also quite capable of making decisions regarding your personal life as well, I just wish you had felt this was information you could have trusted us with sooner. You know, of course, some members of society will frown on your choice of a wife?"

"I am sorry, father, I was afraid you might try to dissuade me from this course and so I acted without your knowledge or blessing and for that I am sorry, and my apologies to you as well, mother," said Richard as he wiped the sweat from his face and what I was sure was also a small tear from his eye.

He really does love her.

"I know some may not approve as you say, but to me the color of Susannah's skin is less important to me than the color of her heart and soul and those are without reproach."

"Richard, your happiness is my most fervent desire, and I can see that you are indeed happy and blessed to have found a woman that you love. You have my full support, my dear," I said, smiling.

"Mine too," said Simon albeit begrudgingly.

The next few months were a whirlwind of getting the couple settled into their new home and we managed it just in time for Susannah to give birth there. Fiona, Amelia, and I gathered when the time came, and as his father had done, Richard wanted to be there to see this new life come into the world and Susannah was happy to have him. The day went as expected, but by nightfall it was clear things were not progressing as they should, and the moaning had turned to screams which rattled us all.

"Richard, I think you should fetch Doctor Snow, we need more expertise here than the three of us can offer," I said quietly so as not to frighten Susannah as she was already quite panicked.

"Is something wrong?"

"No need to worry just yet but I would feel more comfortable if the Doctor were here and he can help with her pain which is most profound, so go hurry now."

Richard left at once and returned very quickly with Doctor Snow following closely behind.

"Step outside everyone except Fiona and Eliza, I need room to work here," he said, getting down to the task at hand.

"Susannah, this is Doctor Snow, he is a family friend, and he is here to help you through this," I said as I wiped her brow with a cool cloth.

She screamed out in pain again as blood began to flow profusely from between her legs and it was only a moment before some laudanum was administered. The screams became faint moans, but it was clear that the birth was still not progressing. We began applying warm compresses to her swollen belly as we massaged her, carefully pushing the baby toward the birth canal hoping for some movement, but nothing seemed to help.

"I am afraid, Eliza, if we do not get this baby out soon, we will lose both baby and mother," said Doctor Snow solemnly.

"Do what you must," I said as I held tightly onto Susannah's hand, Fiona holding the other as I gave her another small sip of the laudanum and she grew quiet.

All we could do now was watch helplessly as the Doctor tried to reach the child to pull it out and I was grateful that Susannah could no longer feel what was being done. After nearly an hour, he was able finally to guide the baby's head out and the body followed quickly, but the poor angel was not breathing, and the little girl was quite blue. Fiona took her and wrapped her in a sheet and laid her next to Susannah. Now we needed to stop the bleeding and we packed her with cotton trying to stem the tide, but they could not contain the red river that continued to flow.

"She will not survive much longer, if you wish to have Richard say his goodbyes now would be the time," said Doctor Snow sadly.

My heart was breaking for him, he had just lost his child and he was about to lose the woman he loved so dearly. We did our best to cover up the bloody sheets before Fiona brought him back into the room.

"Richard, I am sorry but the baby, a little girl, did not survive," I said quietly as he knelt next to the small bundle wrapped up and lying with his wife.

"Susannah?" he asked as tears started to well up in his eyes.

"She is clinging to life but not for much longer, she has lost too much blood and there is nothing more that anyone can do," I said as I placed my hand on his shoulder.

He began to weep, his head on her chest as his body was racked with sobs. She moaned very quietly, and Richard raised his head to speak.

"My darling, I will see you again when my time comes and I will join you and our little girl, in God's grace. Go now and take care of her, my love, I will miss you so," he said as he kissed her gently.

With that, as if waiting for Richard's blessing, Susannah breathed her last and joined her baby girl in heaven. I sent word to Simon to prepare a casket and he and John set quickly to the task. I stayed with Richard who did not want to leave her, and I watched as he held the lifeless body of his daughter in his arms. I knew this pain; I knew this anguish.

Benjamin was a twin, but his brother Joseph survived only a few hours. To lose a child is a type of pain no parent should feel but to lose your wife as well is an agony I cannot imagine.

By sunset, Simon had arrived with the wagon carrying the casket and Amelia was able to convince Richard to go downstairs as Fiona and I set to preparing Susannah and the baby girl who he had named Margareta, to be placed in the casket, mother and baby together. When they were finally ready, Simon, John, Egbert, and Richard carried them downstairs and set the casket in the parlor which Amelia had prepared for that purpose. He sat there all night long and someone from the family always stayed with him. I was there with him during the quiet hours of the morning just before the sun rose.

"How did you do it, mother?" asked Richard quietly.

"Do what, my son?"

"Survive after Simon William died?"

"Ah, yes, your brother," I said as I sighed. "When Simon William was killed, I wondered if I would survive myself. It felt as though the world had collapsed around me, as if the very air that I breathed was gone and I could not get my breath."

"I never understood before how truly painful that must have been for you and father," he said as he looked at me with such a profound sadness it tore at my heart.

"I am sorry that you do now know that pain yourself, it is a pain I would wish on no one least of all my child. Although I thought I would not survive it, I did, and you will too. It will not be the same, your world will always be different, but you will learn to live with the pain and to find a way to go on. Susannah was the most important part of your world, but she was not your whole world, you have your brothers, your sister, your father, and me. We are your world too, and we love you and we are here to help you get through this as best we all can. I did not know Susannah long or well, but I must believe she would want you to find a way to live, live for her, for Margareta."

Richard nodded as the tears flowed again and we sat quietly together as the sun began to peek through the windows, the dawn of another day. You think when something this horrific happens to you that the world cannot possibly continue unchanged since you are changed forever, but it does. The sun rises again whether you want it to or not, and life finds a way, it always does, and it always will.

Sadly, this was not our only loss within the month. Egbert has gone to be with the angels too. Simon can barely remember life without him, and he will be sorely missed. Thankfully, his nephew William has agreed to take his place and we are most grateful to have him, and he joins Ethan who has been working in thc barn these last few years.

Simon has built onto the house to create a larger dining room as our family no longer fits around the table we sat at for so many years. John and Antoinette, Richard, Benjamin, Amelia, and today, Nathaniel finally returns home having completed his studies. He is returning to Boston to join the law practice of a man named Timothy Pickering.

It is wonderful to see him, and as I look around the table I marvel at these young men and women and how far they have come. Amelia is resplendent in the new gown which I just purchased for her and at nearly sixteen she has blossomed into her full beauty. I can walk nowhere with her in town without turning many a redcoat's head. A few men have asked to call on her, but Simon and I have agreed we will wait another year. Richard is still grieving and keeps his own mind about what is going on in Boston, in fact it seems of no consequence to him at all.

I am reveling in seeing my family all gathered but the conversation soon takes the turn I had been dreading.

"Father, I do not think you understand the gravity of what Parliament is trying to do to the colonies, they are being tyrannical in their efforts to control and subjugate us to their will," said Nathaniel forcefully.

"Hear, hear," chimed in Benjamin.

"We are British citizens why should we not be subject to the will of the King?" asked John, clearly confused by his brother's position.

"That is exactly the concern, we are not treated like British citizens, we are treated like "colonists," a lesser man in the eyes of Parliament," responded Nathaniel with venom in his tone.

I could see the storm clouds in his eyes, clearly for him, this was an issue of grave concern indeed. The to and fro between the boys continued for several more minutes before Simon spoke.

"We are British, it is our birthright, our soul, our identity, of that I have no doubt. But Massachusetts and the other colonies have for over one-hundred years now guided their own destiny with little oversight from London. That seems to no longer be the case which we must address."

I could see Nathaniel and Benjamin lean forward expectantly, perhaps thinking they had been persuasive in changing their father's opinion, but Simon was not finished speaking yet.

"Nathaniel and Benjamin, you are right that we deserve to be fully recognized by Parliament and to have the same rights as if we were standing in Saint James Square, but this change must be brought about through peaceful negotiation. These acts of violence, the harassment of Tories it must stop. I cannot, no ... I will not, ever raise my hand against the British government and I would advise all of you to temper your own language and behavior before this escalates further," he said, finally looking solemnly into the faces of his sons.

"Father, I understand what you are asking," said Nathaniel, "but sometimes words are not enough, and they must be followed up with actions. I, for one, am prepared to act to obtain the respect and freedom we deserve."

"If you do so, my son, you will no longer be welcome in this house," said Simon quietly but firmly.

I tried to stifle my gasp, but it escaped before I knew it and the entire table turned in unison to look at me. My eyes locked onto Simon's and the same clouds I had seen in Nathaniel's eyes a few moments ago now appeared in his, a darkness I had never seen before as if he was seeing the future, the turmoil to come.

Yet despite these sometimes-heated discussions that erupted from time to time around us and within, life went on, for us at least, mostly as it always had and the family found a way to coexist, if not without its occasional tensions.

"Mother, do you like the color?" asked Amelia as she whirled around in Mrs. Haines dress shop holding up a pale blue gown against her chest. The color was that of the sky on a clear spring day and perfectly highlighted her pale skin and nearly matched the color of her eyes.

"It is perfection my dear, I think it would be a wonderful choice," I said smiling at her.

A rabbit stole completes the look, the perfect accessory for these cold winter nights. Her first real ball is in just a few weeks, and she has barely been able to contain her excitement. Simon and I have agreed that she may receive callers after this event and so it is a big inflection point in her maturity. She is ready. Calm and poised, beautiful and smart, she is everything I could have ever hoped for in a daughter and more and while still too young to marry she will make a wonderful wife when the time comes.

The night of the ball, Fiona helps me with her hair which shimmers in the candlelight as if it were spun of real gold and as I expected the dress is magnificent on her. Her father and Benjamin await us at the bottom of the stairs, and I watch to see their expressions as she pauses on the landing. The pride in Simon's face is most obvious and Benjamin, with his mouth gaping open, tells me that I am not the only one that thinks she is a beauty. William stands by with our cloaks and Amelia's stole and it is obvious he is also in awe of this beautiful young woman.

The night is sheer perfection and Amelia turns the head of every man in the room, both young and old. Her dance card is filled within just a few minutes of our arrival with no room for more than one dance with any man. Many are clearly disappointed that they did not make it onto her card at all. Josiah's aide-de-camp, Lieutenant Pearson, has earned the coveted first dance and it is obvious that both Simon and Josiah are once again in an alliance much as they were with John and Antoinette. I do not mind; he seems like a very fine young man and his family has been well known to us for many years.

I do not think that Benjamin is as enthusiastic as he dislikes the idea of another British military man in the family, but it is too soon to worry about that. The hours tick away, and I have enjoyed the conversation and the spectacle of it all, but exhaustion is setting in and so Simon and I will head home, leaving Benjamin to chaperone his sister for a few more hours.

"Did you enjoy yourself, my dear," asked Simon as he helped me up into the carriage.

"Very much so, my love, it is a joy to see Amelia so happy and so beautiful."

"She takes after her mother," he said as he kissed me on the cheek, and I could feel the heat rising in my chest.

Simon was just about to climb into the carriage himself when the horses were startled by a noise in the distance, and he stepped back to steady them.

"Easy my boys, easy," he said as he brushed his hand along the muzzle of the dappled gray we called Silverstone. I could hear voices in the distance and the faint glow of torch light beyond the town hall. We waited a few moments, but the voices grew louder and then suddenly two shots echoed through the cold night air, and the voices went quiet.

"Hold here," said Simon to William as he turned to go back into the ballroom. "I am getting the children," he yelled back as he ran away.

Now men were hurrying down the streets having come from the direction of the town hall, many carrying torches as they disappeared into the ale houses and smaller homes. By then, Simon had reappeared with Amelia and Benjamin and many others were following closely behind as the carriages began to fill the streets.

"What is happening?" I asked as he put Amelia into the carriage.

"I am not sure, but it sounds like a protest has gotten out of hand," he said as he climbed up beside me. "Best to be safe and get home quickly." Benjamin hopped up alongside William and picked up the musket that was always kept there as the horses sprang to life and the carriage lurched over the cobblestone streets.

As we turned toward our home, we could see lines of British soldiers moving toward the town square, but we continued toward home without incident. By morning, the grim news had filtered in that a boy, Christopher Seider, had been killed. Ebenezer Richardson, a customs officer, had tried to break up a protest in front of the home of the Tory, Theophilus Lillie, but the angry mob turned on him and followed him to his home. Barricaded inside with his wife and children, the mob began pelting his home with sticks, rocks, and balls of ice, breaking several of the windows. In fear for his life and that of his family, Richardson stuck a musket out of the broken upper window and shot twice into the crowd, hitting young Christopher who died during the night. The boy was not quite twelve.

"This is exactly what I feared," said Simon, shaking his head as if in disbelief as he stared at his morning paper. Nathaniel and Benjamin were silent as they stared down at their full plates, not touching a morsel. Amelia looked teary-eyed as if she would cry at any moment.

"The poor child's mother," I said, feeling my own heart breaking for her.

"No one meant for this boy to be killed," said Nathaniel at last.

"But still a boy is dead!" said Simon, nearly shouting. He removed his spectacles and rubbed his eyes wearily. "I believe you," he finally said more calmly, "but violence leads to violence and Mr. Richardson had every right to protect his family just as I would have done," replied Simon.

"Were you there last night?" I asked Nathaniel, fearful of his reply.

"I was there, mother, but at a distance. I did not participate in the rock throwing, and I did not see the shooting," he said.

"Why Nathaniel, why are you spending your time with … these men?" I asked.

"These men that you seem so disdainful of, mother, are trying to persuade our government officials to treat us as they have treated all Englishmen in these colonies for nearly one-hundred years. Parliament, and the King for that matter, rule by consent of the governed and they are obligated to protect our natural rights."

"That is Pickering talking, you need to be mindful of the man for whom you work, his ideas may not be your own," replied Simon sternly.

"I admire Mr. Pickering," replied Nathaniel as he bit off the corner of his toast, "But these are the ideas of John Locke from the Second Treatise of Government written nearly ninety years ago. Our cause is not a new one, just a new place and time."

Simon leaned back in his chair and crossed his arms across his chest, "What is this "cause" you speak of?" he asked.

"Our natural rights of life, liberty, and property," said Nathaniel bluntly.

"You believe those are being denied to you?"

"We do, father, Parliament is trying to prevent us from having any say over our own destiny or our ability to manage our own affairs as individual colonies as we have always done."

Simon could not muster a response and simply focused on the rest of his meal in silence. Later that day, as the funeral procession wove its way through Boston, hundreds, perhaps thousands, joined in, silently paying their tribute to this little boy and his family. While Simon thought it best to remain at home, I felt compelled to join the crowd and I walked with Nathaniel, Benjamin, and Amelia in silence. The snow was crunching beneath our feet as it began to turn to slush from the sheer volume of those treading the same path. The crowd was quiet, a murmur of hushed conversation and the occasional sound of someone crying were the only noises that filled the bitterly cold air.

The emotions of the day began to wear on my heart, and I felt a tear begin to slide down my face, but it froze onto my cheek, suspended there like a glittering jewel until I pushed it aside with my gloved hand. I did not know this boy or his family, but my heart broke for them, for their loss. But my soul is also filled with dread, a sense of foreboding settled over me which I could not explain. I could see it as sure as I could see the snowflakes swirling around me … death was coming to Boston.

Chapter Four

Death on Our Doorstep

Since the death of the Seider boy, the skirmishes between loyalists and those who saw themselves as Whigs or patriots became more frequent and more violent. It seemed nearly every day that small fights broke out between groups of men or soldiers and patriots angry at the British government. Just today, Sargent Wood had returned to the house with a black eye and scratches across his face from an altercation he had in the street.

I was in the study mending when Nathaniel came in and sat down across from me.

"Mother, I need to speak with you," he said sitting on the edge of his seat, his hands clasped between his knees.

"Go on."

"I am moving out of the house tonight. I am going to be staying at the home of a friend, James Canton, who lives near the town square." My heart sank. I have been fearful of this moment, but it was impossible to believe it would not come.

"Why would you do that? Nathaniel, we have more than enough room for you here." I replied, even though I knew in my heart why he must go.

"Father said that if I choose to act on my convictions, I would no longer be welcome in this house and I am afraid that time has come. I can no longer sit by and be a spectator in current events, it is time to use more than just my voice to effect change," he said quietly but with sincerity.

"Act how?" I asked, my heart beating a bit faster.

"Mother I cannot tell you more. I do not want to put you in an awkward position with father and for your own safety it is best you not know more."

"And what of your safety?"

"There comes a time, mother, when men must stand by their beliefs. They must stand up for themselves, for those whose voices are weak. That time has come and there are risks that must be taken..." he trailed off.

I pulled my shawl tightly around my shoulders, but it did not keep out the cold I could feel seeping up my arms and engulfing me in its unwelcome embrace.

"Have you spoken to your father? Surely he did not mean it when he said you would not be welcome here. He was upset."

"I have and he is firm and has as much of a right to his convictions as I do to mine, and I will not disrespect him by staying in his home. A change is coming, mother, and sides will be chosen whether we like it or not."

He was right of course; we have all seen it coming. Much like a storm you see in the distance as it roils across the open fields, the dark clouds keep moving toward you, until suddenly you realize there is no escape and that the storm will engulf you.

"You will stay in communication with me?"

"I will, mother, and I promise I will do my best to keep you and the family out of my dealings, but

I must be true now to my own heart," he said as he came and knelt before me.

I brushed back the thick dark hair from his forehead, he looked so much like Simon William now, gone nearly ten years. I could not bear the sorrow of losing another son, but I respected his decision despite the pain it was causing.

"Be safe my son, and when this difficulty has passed, we will be together as a family again," I said as I kissed him on each cheek and held him in a tight embrace.

"I hope you are right, mother; I pray you are right," he whispered in my ear before he turned to go.

I watched as the flames died in the grate, but I did not have the strength to tend to them and William was not nearby. I could hear Fiona singing in the kitchen and Amelia and Benjamin chattering in the study. It all seemed so familiar, so comforting and yet so strange. In the course of life, you expect there to be conflicts, wars even. And you know that there is a chance those conflicts will take a toll on your own family. We lost Simon William in defense of this land against the French and others that we have known and cared for have died defending it. What I never imagined in my life was that my family might be at war with itself.

I shivered, not because the fire was low but because for the first time in my life I was frightened, truly frightened to my very soul. Surely Nathaniel would never raise his hand against this family … would he?

Benjamin and Amelia never spoke of Nathaniel's departure, but our meals were a much quieter and subdued affair. Street fighting has become more and more common, scuffles between small groups of men who disagree with each other about British rule.

Vandals and ruffians have been painting large white letter T's on windows branding homes and businesses as those belonging to Tories. It is hard to imagine that being loyal to King and Crown is now something to be mocked and ridiculed. Our home has been spared but the warehouse I am told was painted on every window. None of the women are now allowed to leave the house without a male escort with them, preferably armed.

True to his word, Nathaniel has sent me a post every week or so. I have not shared them with Simon, nor does he ask if I have heard from him. He is stoic on the matter, but I can see that it hurts him to be separated from his son and he has taken no pleasure in it. The weather continues to be quite cold and many thought that would keep the skirmishes at bay, but it seems to have been no deterrent. It is a dark and moonless evening and Simon has gone down to the warehouse with John to see about a report of some broken windows.

"Benjamin, where are you going?" I called out from the parlor, catching a glimpse of him heading into the kitchen bundled up with a coat and scarf. He paused and turned back to me.

"I am meeting with Nathaniel, mother," he said, almost more of a question than a statement.

"Does your father know?"

"I have not spoken to him on this matter, will you tell him?"

I know Simon would not approve but to keep them apart, brothers who share the same flesh and blood, does not seem fair either.

"No, I will not mention it, but if he asks me directly, you know I will not lie to him, or to any man, on your behalf," I said finally.

"Thank you," replied Benjamin as he quickly scurried out the door before I could change my mind.

I sat reading for a while hoping Benjamin would return before his father. Keeping things from my husband is not ideal, and it gave me a sense of unease that hung over me like a heavy weight bearing down on me and making it difficult to breathe. I love my husband beyond measure, and my children, but now I find myself walking this line between them, Simon, and John on one side and Nathaniel and Benjamin on the other. I see the value in the arguments on both sides, but more importantly, I see the value in them, none more than the other and I want nothing more than for my family to be whole.

In the distance I begin to hear bells ringing outside, normally a call to fight a fire but as I look out the window, I see no glow in the sky. Sargent Wood clamors down the stairs fully dressed and dashes out of the front door without a word. I ring for William.

"William, is there a fire?" I inquired.

"No, Mrs. Parkman, I believe that is an alarm call from the British headquarters," he replied looking rattled.

I could feel my heart racing, clearly there was trouble, and somewhere in that trouble were my two sons no doubt. As I continue to peer out into the darkness, I can see men and even a few women beginning to fill the streets headed toward the Customs House. If Simon were here, surely he would go but at the warehouse he may be too far from town to realize what is happening.

I ran quickly up the stairs and threw on a heavier dress and warmer shoes and I tied my hair up in a scarf. "William, grab my cloak please," I shouted on my way back down.

"Mrs. Parkman, what are you doing? You cannot go out there, Master Simon would never forgive me if I let you go," he said, his voice rising higher than I had ever heard it before. William certainly lacked Egbert's decorum because I never heard his voice change in tone or pitch.

"William, I am going and if you feel compelled to accompany me you may, but I am going," I repeated and with that I was out the door before he even had time to react. It took him only a minute or so to catch up with me, now heavily wrapped in a cloak with a scarf across his face.

"Mrs. Parkman, please, please, come back to the house," he said as he tried to grab my arm.

"No, William, my sons may be out here, and they may need our help," I said, determined to keep moving.

A large crowd had formed outside the Customs House, the place where the Crown kept its money. I pushed my way to the front, all the while scanning the faces for signs of Nathaniel and Benjamin. These were men and women that I knew. Their faces though were filled with anger, and a hatred that I had not seen before, and it frightened me. Perhaps William was right, maybe I should leave and return home. I do not know why I felt so strongly that they were here and in danger, but it was a feeling that would not be ignored. I moved more to the side, closer to where I could see a British soldier guarding the entrance. I recognized him as Private White who I had met when he accompanied Sargent Wood on one occasion.

The poor boy was clearly frightened, the mob pelting him with rocks and snowballs, but he held his ground holding tightly onto his musket which he held across his chest. Many in the crowd were shouting obscenities at him and their words made me blush. The bells were still pealing and very quickly Captain Thomas Preston and a half dozen or so of his officers joined Private White and formed a barricade across the fence to the Customs House.

The crowd shifted and moved, getting closer to the men, then retreating a bit, undulating like a snake does in the grass. Finally, across the square I could see one of the figures I had been searching for, it was Nathaniel, but I did not see Benjamin with him, and he was now too far away for me to get to him easily. The crowd was beginning to fracture in its sentiments, some trying to goad the soldiers into action, others trying to calm the situation. I could see Nathaniel but could not tell for sure of which mind he might be but as he went from man to man he seemed to be gesturing for restraint and calm. The shouting was louder now, men and women's voices raised in anger and frustration echoed off the buildings of the square.

The soldiers raised their muskets as the crowd grew closer, "Do not fire," I could hear Captain Preston shouting above the fray.

"I repeat, do not fire," he said again as loudly as he could.

I could hear the fear in his voice, the concern and it shook me to my core. This situation seemed to be barely under control when two men with clubs approached the line and began to hit the soldiers standing there, and more fell in behind them flinging rocks and ice. I could hear men in the crowd yelling "no, get back, do not approach them," but it was too late. The next sound I heard was a shot fired so close to me that I could feel the vibrations within my body. Next, several more shots rang out and the people started fleeing in every direction. I sank down to my knees with William shielding me with his body as chaos ensued around us.

"We must leave now," said William as he grabbed firmly onto my arm, but I rose and twisted away from him, running toward the place I had last seen Nathaniel. The air was filled with smoke that swirled around me creating a haze that made it hard to see. I could tell there were bodies lying in the square while others leaned over them trying to render aid. For some, it was clear that it was already too late. Men and women were shouting, and I could hear a woman wailing as she knelt over the body of one of the men now lying in a pool of his own blood. My heart was racing as I searched frantically for my son among those lying wounded and dead in the snow.

Finally, I saw him, he was kneeling on the ground, but I could not tell if he was hurt. I picked my way carefully among those lying in the square and now I was close enough to see that Nathaniel was tending to a man named Samuel Evans. He was well known to our family and he and Nathaniel had been friends since they were children, but now he lay in the snow covered in blood and mud.

There was a gaping hole in the side of his chest and arm. Nathaniel was doing his best to stem the red tide that was trickling into the cracks of the cobblestones and turning the snow to a crimson red. I quickly removed my scarf. "Here, tie this around his arm," I said as I handed it to Nathaniel. The shock on his face was obvious but rather than question my presence he grabbed the scarf and began tying it around Samuel's arm.

"Are you hurt? Where is Benjamin?" I asked frantically.

"No, I am not hurt, this blood is not mine, and he is not here. I made him go home when it was clear there would be trouble, and you should not be here either mother, what were you thinking coming here?" he shouted at me, clearly angered.

"I was thinking of you, of your brother, and I feared that you might be in danger, and I had to come."

"I cannot believe father let you leave," he said as he tried to sit Samuel up.

"Your father is at the warehouse with John. I came on my own accord."

"Let me help you," said William as he took Samuel's other arm and helped hoist him from the cold wet ground.

"She should not be here, William," he said tersely.

"I know sir, I am sorry, but your mother can be most obstinate when she wishes to be," he replied breathlessly, grunting from the effort of getting Samuel off the ground.

"Over here, we can take him to Dr. Warren's house," said Nathaniel as he flung the almost lifeless man over his shoulder and started off to just a few doors down the street. There were still many people filling the streets, some still shouting after the soldiers who had moved inside the fence and out of harm's way. William took the lead pushing people out of the way as Nathaniel labored under the weight of his friend. There was a crowd of people already inside and some with more minor wounds waiting on the street.

"Wait here," commanded Nathaniel as he and William took Samuel inside.

The crowd gathered outside Dr. Warren's house waited quietly but I felt the people staring, wondering why I should be here, in this place at this time. Many know me, and they know my husband to be a true friend to the Crown. They were right to wonder, as I did not really know myself, other than the force that possesses a mother when she fears for her child propelling me to this place. My dress was covered in mud, wet from the snow and sticky with blood, which also covered my hands. I did my best to wipe them on the hem of the dress I was wearing underneath my cloak. It seemed like an eternity before Nathaniel emerged again, but I am sure it was only a few minutes.

"You have to go, now, go home at once," said Nathaniel as he and William emerged from the doctor's home.

"Samuel?"

"He is dead, mother, go home…"

William and I practically ran through the streets, my tears flowing freely as the gravity of what had just happened began to sink in. Benjamin and Fiona were waiting for us when we returned, and we quickly changed out of our clothes which they whisked away while William and I cleaned up. Surely, Simon would be home at any moment. What was I going to say? I scraped the dried blood and mud from underneath my fingernails as Fiona took down my hair and began to brush it out, deftly removing the remnants of this horrible evening.

Men had been killed tonight, men we knew, how many I could not say for certain. Their blood was on my hands, on the hands of the soldiers who fired, and on the hands of those who perhaps gave them no choice but to defend themselves. I drank the brandy that Benjamin brought me, but thankfully he asked me no questions and retreated to his room, not anxious to face his father either.

"Thank you, Fiona, I think that will be enough," I said as I squeezed her hand. "We will not speak of this with Master Simon, yes?"

"Of course, ma'am, I am just grateful that you and the boys are not hurt. I will go and see what can be done with your dress."

I pulled the chair in my bedchamber closer to the fire, but I could still feel the cold as if I were standing in that square. The men were so ferociously angry, as if years of pent-up feelings had found their way to the surface and could no longer be kept in. I could sense their emotions in that moment, and I do not think it is a feeling I will ever forget. I have seen death before, but I have never seen men cut down by musket in front of my very eyes. My hands were shaking, and I felt sick…

Simon, thankfully, did not return until the wee hours of the morning, and I was already asleep. The accounts in the paper were both horrifying in their detail and slanted depending on whose side of the tragedy they took. The Boston Massacre, some papers were already calling it. Five men lost their lives, Crispus Attucks a mixed-race man, Samuel Gray a rope maker, sailor James Caldwell, Patrick Carr, and of course Samuel Evans. Nearly a dozen more were wounded. Captain Preston and his men have been arrested but it is unclear if that is more for their protection than for their guilt.

Some say he gave the order to shoot, others say it was someone in the crowd who yelled "fire" to bring on the attack to justify their outrage and resistance. I for one never heard the British order to fire but, in the chaos, it is impossible to know for sure. Simon did not seem to be aware that anything was amiss, and Benjamin and I did not speak of it. In fact, I never spoke of it to anyone, ever.

It was many more months before Captain Preston and his men went to trial and, surprisingly, they were defended by John Adams who was an outspoken critic of the British government, but also a man who believed in the law and their right to receive a fair trial. Nathaniel and James Pickering were often at the courthouse in support of Mr. Adams according to the papers. Many were pushing for the death penalty for these men, and it was only fair that they be defended as vigorously as any citizen of Boston. God knows, this town needs no more blood on its hands.

Many eyewitnesses testified at the proceedings, but each seemed to contradict the last. Adams successfully argued that there was reasonable doubt and Preston was found not guilty. Two of the soldiers claimed self-defense and they were also found not guilty, and two others—Hugh Montgomery and Matthew Kilroy, were found guilty of manslaughter and were branded on the thumbs as first offenders under British law.

While some felt justice had been done, many were not so sure. Either way, to keep the peace, Governor Hutchinson ordered the withdrawal of troops from some of the barracks in Boston proper to Castle William, an island he believed would provide more effectively for their safety. While there were fewer soldiers roaming the streets of Boston, make no mistake that King George III continued to add to the number of soldiers stationed in Massachusetts. Ships came every few weeks with more and more soldiers. Soon it seemed, there were nearly as many soldiers as there were citizens. If there was going to be a fight, the King was going to be ready.

Chapter Five

Tighten the Noose

The months slip quietly away and become years before you even realize they have gone. My mother often said that time seemed to move more quickly as she aged. I think when one compares themselves to their children and grandchildren, the passage of time does indeed seem to march on at a faster pace than it did when we were young. Amelia has been receiving callers for some time now, but none seem to have garnered much interest on her part. She has taken on tutoring French for a few of the girls from the academy run by Mr. Burton which she previously attended. Her French is spoken beautifully, and she is happy to be able to use it a few times each week. Benjamin is, I think, interested in one of the young ladies so it is an arrangement that works well for them both.

It has been nearly two years since the Boston Massacre, but the anger still simmers as if it were yesterday. More and more the English government tries to rein in the colonies despite the constant resistance. A few months ago, Parliament passed the Tea Act to try to reduce the enormous amount of tea in the stores of the British East India Company which has been struggling for some time. Parliament knew if they could undercut the price of tea being smuggled in to avoid taxes, that colonists would purchase Company tea, which of course meant Townshend duties would be paid. But in purchasing Company tea colonists also knew that they were acknowledging Parliament's right to tax the colonies, the very issue that had started so much of the quarrel for these few years.

Not so easily outsmarted, a coalition of merchants and smugglers mobilized to thwart delivery and distribution of the tea, harassing ships, and preventing much of the tea from being delivered. This new tension only serves to further cause angry discourse and social events and even simple visits have become less frequent as people have become more and more reluctant to venture from the safety of their homes. But I am pleased to see Mary Welles today for tea as I have not seen her for some time.

"I am returning to London," said Mary as her tea-cup rattled slightly in its saucer. She has begun to show her age and her hand is less steady than in years past.

"Mary, I am so surprised, you seem so happy here in Boston?"

"Boston has been wonderful to me, but it is no longer the place it was when I first arrived, and I no longer feel ... safe," she responded with a sigh.

"Has something happened?"

"No, no, nothing of particular note but it is clear to me that this angst, this divide between colonists and the Crown is continuing to grow, and I see no end to it that bodes well for the Colonies," she said, shaking her head from side to side. "No, this will not end well, I am afraid," she said as she helped herself to another biscuit. "You will stay?" she asked.

I could not have been more shocked than if she had struck me in the face with her hand and it took me a moment to speak.

"Of course I will stay, this is my home, Mary, I could never leave," I said as I stared at her in disbelief.

"I understand, but it is not mine, my home is England, and it is to England I will go."

"I'm sorry that you feel you must leave, and I wish you nothing but health and happiness, but for me, Boston is my home. The home of my mother and grandmother and I could never leave it."

"You are a true colonist," she replied smiling.

"I am loyal to the Crown make no mistake on it," I replied quickly.

"Of that I have no doubt my dear, but you are not English as I am, you are of this place, of this time, and I suppose it is right for you to stay," she said with a bit of an air of superiority, and in that moment, I felt a bit like the oft-lamented "second-class citizen" Benjamin frequently spoke of.

After Mary left, I could not help but think about our conversation. Who am I really? Am I an English woman or a colonist and can I be both? This land beneath my feet has been home to my family for one-hundred-and-fifty-years. I have been to England two or three times for perhaps a total of three months ...

so is England really where my loyalty should lie? I glanced around the empty room grateful to see there was no one nearby who might be able to intercept my thoughts. I was not even sure myself what I was thinking. Are Nathaniel and Benjamin, and so many others, right? Should we be treated more as equals, with more say in our own governance than Parliament and the King want to allow?

These past few years have taken a horrible toll on our family and the divide Mary spoke of is evident at my own dinner table around which Nathaniel no longer sits. Benjamin keeps his counsel to himself, but I know he is very sympathetic to his brother's cause. John is adamant that the Crown must be defended at all costs. Richard and Amelia seem to do their best to straddle the divide as I have. Simon, while loyal to the Crown, does not seem to take the hard stance that John does, perhaps because he knows doing so would further alienate Nathaniel and Benjamin.

But now, perhaps for the first time, I am starting to wonder if my own mind is more with the colonists than I first believed. I shake my head as if trying to physically remove the idea from my very thoughts.

My husband is loyal to the Crown, and so must I be, but … if I am true to myself, I have felt the feelings within me growing over time and I know not how much longer I can live before falling into the depths of this divide knowing not where I might land.

Mary is not the only one leaving, others have gone too and now Richard has decided to return to Barbados before winter sets in and the journey becomes too harsh, he wants no part of this drama which continues to unfold in Boston on a nearly daily basis. I shall miss him, but I must conclude that it is not likely I will ever see him again and it pains my heart so. With winter coming on my thoughts are most melancholy indeed and even Simon has noticed.

"My dear, perhaps we should host a Christmas party this year, what do you think?" asked Simon over a dinner of roast mutton and leeks.

"Oh, could we mother, could we?" said Amelia, her eyes brightly shimmering in the candlelight. Even Benjamin seemed to perk up at the thought of it.

"I think that would be a splendid idea," I replied.

Amelia leapt from her seat and practically danced around the table as she kissed her father and I in turn, before running up the stairs to see "if I should have anything suitable to wear."

Simon was right, a party is just what everyone needs, life has been too dull, and too difficult of late and some gaiety is needed by all.

Fiona and I spent the next month working out the details and invitations were finally sent out for the December 16th gathering which we have decided to host at the warehouse, one whole side of which has been empty for months. We can decorate in the holiday spirit and host at least one hundred guests there; it will be the event of the holiday season.

Benjamin and Amelia helped to gather holly and laurel with which to decorate, and Fiona brought in two extra girls to help with the baking and preparations. Amelia and I bought new gowns, hers with threads of bright red and gold and mine with strands of silver to match my hair which is now more grey than brown.

The night of the party broke cold and a bit snowy and damp, but spirits were high as people flooded into the warehouse. I was so pleased at how the decorating had been done and the room, once filled with people dressed in their finest clothes, shone like a brilliant gemstone. A trio of musicians provided beautiful music and it echoed through the space in the most wonderful way. Fiona had outdone herself with the food, and the wine and rum flowed freely. I have even gotten Simon to agree that Nathaniel could attend given that the party was not going to be held in our home. I have not seen him since that night in the square except at church where we would speak briefly in passing.

The shuffling of the dancers' feet in time to the music reverberated off the high ceilings as the candlelight turned the dancers to shadows moving across the walls. The smell of the wooden casks filled the room punctuated by the boughs of fresh greens. Josiah was there with a dozen or so of his soldiers, but mostly friends and business acquaintances of Simon and their adult children. Amelia and Benjamin seemed to be having a grand time as did John and Antoinette. It did my heart so much good to see people having a good time and I was so happy we had chosen to do this.

"Good evening, mother," said a familiar voice over my shoulder and I turned to find Nathaniel in his finest suit sporting a large grin.

"My darling son how good to see you," I said as I hugged him close to me. "Have you seen your father?"

"No not yet, but I have greeted Amelia and Benjamin," he said smiling. "She is a real beauty, mother, just like you."

"She most certainly is," I said with less humility than was probably appropriate.

"Nathaniel," said Simon as we both turned around to find him standing behind us.

"Father, it is good to see you," said Nathaniel as he put out his hand.

My heart caught in my throat, but I need not fear, whatever issues Simon might have at this moment Nathaniel was not just our son he was our guest, and he extended his own hand to shake his. They looked so much alike these two, Nathaniel probably more than any of the boys was the spitting image of his father, in appearance at least.

"You look well, are you still keeping with Mr. Pickering," he asked.

"No, father, I went to work with John Adams a few months ago. He is a very wise and learned man and I have grown much in my understanding of the law under his guidance," replied Nathaniel.

Simon clearly was not aware but seemed to be pleased.

"He is an honorable man of fine character son, and you are well to be associated with him," he replied somewhat surprisingly. While Mr. Adams had defended Captain Preston and his men after the Boston Massacre it was clear he was on the side of the patriots.

"Thank you, father, I am pleased that you approve."

And with that, the exchange was over, Simon moved on to speak with other guests, but it did my heart good to see this civil interaction between them. Perhaps the divide was not as large as I feared. After several hours of merriment, the party was winding down as we said good night to the last of our guests and waved as the final carriage pulled away.

"I am weary to the bone," I told Simon as he helped me with my cloak.

"Well, you were a wonderful hostess and I believe a grand time was had by all. I know I enjoyed myself thoroughly."

"It was nice to see so many friends, was it not?"

"Indeed, and it was good to see Nathaniel," replied Simon as he helped me into the carriage.

I smiled. I knew Simon would not be harsh with him forever, perhaps there was a thawing in this icy relationship. As we headed north along the wharf there seemed to be more people than usual out at this time of night, especially in the winter. As we rounded the corner toward Boston Harbor it was clear something was happening, as there was a large but mostly silent crowd gathered along the water's edge near where the *Dartmouth, Eleanor,* and *Beaver* were docked. The *Dartmouth* has for the last few weeks been the subject of much debate as protests have erupted led by Samuel Adams and his followers, the Sons of Liberty, as they attempted to prevent them from unloading their cargo of tea.

To accept the tea was to accept the tax and many were unwilling to do so. A meeting was held just a couple of weeks ago which was widely attended, even Simon and John were there, as Governor Hutchinson took a stand and demanded that the ships be allowed to unload their cargo. After all, two of the three ships' Captains were his sons, and it would be an embarrassment to him personally if these rebels successfully interrupted the flow of tea from England.

But the protestors were having none of it and they had set men to watch the ships to be sure they did not unload their cargo. But why were so many gathered here on this cold dark night?

"William, pull up here," said Simon as he opened the door and stepped out onto the wharf. Despite his request that I stay in the carriage, I followed him out and from our vantage point I could see what the crowd was watching. There were men, perhaps a hundred or so of them, most dressed as Indians, I say this because it was clear that it was a pretense, men with charcoal on their faces and feathers in their hats.

They were onboard the ships, and they were quickly but methodically hacking open the tea chests and dumping their contents into Boston Harbor. The crowd watched quietly as the "Indians" went about their work. I looked around to see if there were red-coats who might intervene, but I saw no one and Hutchinson had posted no guards here, perhaps hoping to avoid a conflict with the protestors.

Simon and I watched silently for a few minutes when I caught a clear look at one of the men throwing tea from the bow on the *Eleanor* which was closest to where we had stopped. The clouds have moved away from the moon just enough to shed more light on the scene playing out before us. The man seemed familiar but, in the darkness, it was … I felt Simon stiffen. It was Nathaniel.

"Get in the carriage," said Simon brusquely.

I could not imagine the hurt he was feeling, and he said nothing on the way home but after Fiona left us in our room, I could hold it in no longer.

"Simon, I know you are upset with Nathaniel, but even though we may not agree with his choices he is still our son."

"Choices? He is committing treason, Eliza, do you think that will go unpunished?"

"Surely they cannot punish all of them, there must have been a hundred men on those ships."

"Admiral Montagu's men were watching, Eliza, and even if they do not arrest those men there will be consequences. I am sure the only reason they did not intervene was to avoid endangering the lives of the people standing on the wharf who were doing no wrong, but mark my words, this will not stand."

"Will they arrest Nathaniel?"

"I do not know," said Simon with a weary sigh.

As if foretelling the very future, Simon's words came to bear and it was only a few months before Parliament began enforcing new laws meant to bring Boston to heel. Soon the Royal Navy blockaded the port so his Majesty's commerce could take place without fear of interference or destruction. They also allowed no exports to foreign ports and the only imports allowed were provisions for the British Army as well as necessaries such as wheat. The King made it clear that the port would stay shuttered until Bostonians made restitution to the East India Company. Not even Simon's rum was permitted.

But that was not all, the Massachusetts Government Act was next, and it effectively destroyed our ability to elect our own representatives to the Massachusetts Council as we always had, instead giving that authority to the governor and the Council was formed of men appointed by the crown. The Governor could now also choose judges, county sheriffs, and jurors and limit town meetings to just once a year without prior government approval.

Boston was now in peril of its very life and the Crown was tightening the noose.

Chapter Six

A Spy Among Us

While most of Parliament's attacks were aimed at Boston and Massachusetts, it was clear that all the Colonies were concerned about these developments and in response the First Continental Congress was held in September with the goal of expressing concerns to Parliament as well as calling for a boycott of British imports. I have never seen Simon so concerned and it is clear that our livelihood is in jeopardy.

"Father, I think we should sell the north warehouse," said John as we gathered for a dinner which included Josiah Hutton.

"Why would we do such a thing?" I asked John quizzically.

"We cannot afford to keep all this empty space, mother, and we are going to need to generate some income soon," was his terse reply.

"But surely this is temporary is it not?"

Simon shook his head, "No, I do not think it is temporary. I think John is right, we are going to have to consider some other means of supporting the family. It may be a very long time before the harbor opens again."

"Now Simon, the harbor will open soon, it has to," I said with a nervous laugh.

"Eliza, the King has been very clear on this issue, without full restitution for the tea the harbor will remain closed. I am sorry this is having such a negative impact on this family, but it must be done," replied Josiah.

"I think you are right, John, let us see about selling the north warehouse, we have to generate some income for the family, and this may be the best way."

"I have another suggestion," said Josiah glancing up from the table to look at John. "Take a commission with the army. We are looking to add more officers, preferably Boston natives who know the community and its leaders."

"You mean spies," said Benjamin, not hiding his disdain.

"That is not what I meant," said Josiah defensively.

"No, but it is what you intend to accomplish is it not?"

"Enough Benjamin, Josiah is a part of this family, and I will not have you insult him in our home," said Simon sternly. "John, you might consider taking Josiah up on his offer as there is little to do now, and it would ease the burden a bit."

"I would be honored," said John.

And with a handshake, it was done. Another Parkman son was to put on the regimental uniform of the British Army and while I did not fear for his safety, I feared it would further fracture the family. Already I could see the storm clouds gathering over Benjamin as he scowled at John.

"Brother, tell me why you would want to join the oppressors against those who are only asking to be treated as full citizens in charge of their own destiny," said Benjamin, more calmly than I expected.

"I see, dear brother, that you have been spending too much time with Nathaniel."

"No, I have been spending time with the writings of Samuel Adams and John Dickinson and reading the reports from the Continental Congress. I have been educating myself as all good citizens of Boston should do. We have petitioned, we have begged the Crown and asked for its intersession to stop the tyranny of Parliament, but we are ignored, our remonstrances have been met with hatred and insult, and our requests have been disregarded and held in contempt," he said with a passion I have never heard him speak with before.

"What are you suggesting should be done?" I asked.

"We want to make our own way and decide for ourselves with whom we trade and how we best govern. Those decisions should not be made by men thousands of miles away. Hope of reconciliation has been lost. If we wish to be free to preserve the liberties for which we have been fighting, we must pledge ourselves to the struggle until the object of our desire has been won."

"This is not a war Benjamin," chided John.

"It might be…" said Benjamin, looking directly at Josiah.

"I can see that you feel very ardently, Ben," said Josiah. "But the British are not your enemies, we are of the same blood, the same heritage."

"Are we?" he replied.

Josiah thought it best not to respond and for that I was grateful. There was more than enough of this conversation for one night, but I was struck by Benjamin's passion and eloquence on this matter, and I could feel within my own heart that his words rang true and sincere.

That night after everyone had gone, Simon and I sat in the study in front of the fire, much as we had done the night we buried Simon William, and over the room hung the same pall, this feeling of sorrow and remorse. My family was at odds with itself, and I did not know how much longer we would survive.

"Simon, what are we going to do about the children?"

"They are not children, Eliza, they are grown men and women entitled to their own thoughts and opinions," he said with a sigh.

"Surely you do not agree with Benjamin that war is coming?"

Simon leaned back in his chair and closed his eyes for a moment. I could see the weariness in him, his face gaunt, his hair now nearly all gray, his age becoming more apparent. The pressures of all of this have taken a toll on him, it is true.

"It is already here," he said matter-of-factly.

"Whatever do you mean?" I asked, the alarm rising in my voice.

"Governor Gage is consolidating his troops here in Boston and he is stockpiling weapons and gunpowder. There have already been confrontations between militia and British troops and while they have not resulted in gunfire, it is only a matter of time."

"But the militia are here for our defense, surely they will not become an army against the British?" I said, feeling my heart beating faster.

"That is exactly what they will do. I have heard they are also stockpiling weapons and powder of their own near Lexington. Gage is going to have no choice, sooner or later he will have to take control."

"Simon, we cannot allow John to join the Regiment, what if he is faced with…"

"I know, my dear, it is heavy on my soul that our sons may be poised on the battlefield with their muskets aimed at each other, but I do not see how we can prevent it. Nathaniel has thrown his lot in with the Patriots and John will remain loyal to the crown. Now, I do not know how far Benjamin will take his beliefs, but I've no doubt he supports the cause."

The tears began to trickle down my cheeks and I had no desire to stop them. My heart was tearing in two, how could this be happening, how could it be that brother will fight against brother? All I could do was pray fervently that Simon was wrong, and that bloodshed could be avoided.

We have sold the north warehouse as John had suggested and the other sits nearly empty now as the blockade persists. Simon now spends more and more of his time at the meetinghouse listening to the ever-increasing pitch of the rhetoric from both sides. Tempers are flaring and signs of the coming conflict are all around. Despite my protests, Benjamin has moved out of our home and is living with Nathaniel. John has assumed his position as Captain in Josiah's regiment and since he is spending most of his days, and many of his nights at their headquarters, we thought it best that Antoinette and the children stay with us, and it has warmed my heart to have young children in the house again.

Simon has invited Governor Gage and his lovely wife, Margaret, to join us for dinner on Saturday along with General Clinton and his wife, Josiah, and of course John, Antoinette, and Amelia. We had Governor Hutchinson in our home many times, but I have not had the pleasure of meeting Governor Gage although I have met his wife several times. Like me, Margaret was born in the colonies, her father was a wealthy businessman and politician in the province of New Jersey, and I find her to be both witty and charming.

Dinner was a lively affair, and I was grateful that there was almost no talk of the issues of the day but instead we talked of music and art and all of the things that make Boston such a wonderful place to live. I found the Governor to be rather stodgy and direct but General Clinton was a wonderful story-teller and he kept the group entertained with his adventures. When the men retreated to the study for whiskey, the women gathered in the parlor for tea, which Margaret was kind enough to supply.

"These are trying times indeed are they not?" asked Margaret as she settled her ample frame into the overstuffed chair closest to the fire. She was a pretty woman, her dark hair perfectly coifed, her cor-set straining to keep her upright.

"They are indeed," said Antoinette as she blew gently on the precious contents of her china cup.

"Mrs. Gage are you finding Boston to your lik-ing?" asked Amelia politely.

"Indeed, it is a wonderful city. Truly dear, I enjoy it here very much although I cannot say that my husband feels the same. I think he would have preferred to stay in London."

"I am sorry to hear your husband does not like it here," I replied.

"It is not the city per se that he does not like, it is the roguish element of the town which persists in

these efforts to taunt and harangue the British government which pushes him to the limits of his patience."

"I can certainly understand how that might happen," said Antoinette, "John complains most vigorously that the actions of the few are taking such a
terrible toll on all of us."

"It is no longer just a few I am afraid, the ranks
of the disenchanted and rebellious grow by leaps and
bounds every day," replied Amelia.

I wondered if Margaret would mention Nathaniel
and I glanced nervously at Amelia who appeared to
be thinking the same thing, but she made no mention
of him directly.

"This Samuel Adams fellow is a compelling
writer and speaker, and he has ignited a spirit I have
never seen before in the colonies," said Margaret
thoughtfully.

"He has indeed, he feels quite passionately about
his desire for equality and liberty," I added.

"I believe Mr. Adams and the men of the
Continental Congress have the best interests of the
colonies at heart, even if I do not always agree with
their methods," Margaret added.

I was taken aback by her words, she seems to be almost sympathetic to their cause, not at all what I would have expected from the wife of the man the Crown has sent here to quash any rebellion.

"Well, it will be resolved in the next few days, and I think life in Boston will begin to find a sense of normalcy again," she said as she drained her cup.

"Here, permit me, Mrs. Gage," said Amelia as she stepped up to pour another for her. "You were saying, things are about to change?'

"Yes, although I must not say much more, but the Governor and his Generals have it in hand and they are leaving tomorrow to put this to rest."

"John did not mention he was leaving tomor-row?" said Antoinette.

"He may not know yet dear, it is all very hush-hush of course."

After that the conversation turned to other things and the evening ended on a pleasant note, and Amelia and I helped Fiona clear the tea service before I headed up to bed. Simon and John were still in the study with Josiah, but I thought it best not to wait up.

"Amelia, are you coming up?

"In a minute mother, I have a small spot on my dress I want to see if I can get out before I retire."

"Very well my dearest," I said, kissing her on the cheek.

Fiona came up to take down my hair, but I realized I had not paid my respects to Josiah.

"One moment, Fiona, I will need to say good-night to Josiah."

"Oh, ma'am, I am sure the Major will not mind if you do not go back down," she replied with a bit of a nervous laugh.

"Fiona, why would you suggest such a thing, it would be the height of rudeness," I said as I made my way down the stairs.

After saying goodnight to Josiah, I was just about to go up the stairs to my room when I heard a noise in the kitchen. Surely Fiona was still waiting for me, and William was waiting near the study should the men need anything further. I ventured into the kitchen, startled to find Amelia by the back door wearing her cloak.

"Amelia, what are you doing?"

"Oh, mother, you frightened me," she said as she looked around, her eyes wide and her cheeks flushed.

"Why are you wearing your cloak?"

"I need to … go out," she said bluntly.

I found myself whispering now as it was clear that whatever was going on it was probably best that the men not become aware.

"Amelia, you cannot go out alone. What would compel you to leave the house at this hour?" I hissed at her in the dim light.

"I cannot say."

"You cannot say, or you will not say? Either way, this is not acceptable, Amelia."

She looked down at the floor as she wrung her hands together.

"I need to speak to Nathaniel…"

"Well, that may be but surely it can wait until tomorrow."

"No mother, it cannot."

I stared at my daughter as a realization started to sink in.

"This is about what Margaret, Mrs. Gage, said is it not?"

"Yes."

"Amelia, Amelia," I said as I drew her close to me.

"You want to warn your brothers that something is happening?"

"I have to mother; they have to know or else all may be lost."

"All of what may be lost, my dear?" I said gently.

"Everything they have been working for these past months. Now I have to go mother, please, I have no time to waste."

My heart caught in my throat. Perhaps if she told Nathaniel, it would avoid a conflict that could see my sons pitted against each other. I bit into my upper lip, nearly drawing blood as I pondered what to do. There was no way I could go with her, and I did not trust William not to tell Simon.

"You cannot go alone, I will send Fiona down to go with you, but be quick about it and make no noise when you return."

"Thank you, mother," she said as she kissed me on the forehead.

"Do not thank me, if your father learns of this, I do not know what the consequences will be. I cannot say I fully understand why you must do this but if you must go, be safe and give my love to your brothers."

With that I turned and hurried upstairs. Fiona must have already known what Amelia was up to as she said nothing when I sent her down. Clearly, she had been trying to keep me in my room earlier, no doubt to prevent me from stumbling onto Amelia before she could depart. Whatever was going on they were in on it together. My stomach churned and my mind was a whirl thinking about what was happening. I brushed quickly through my hair, focusing on every stroke as I tried to calm my breathing. The door opened, startling me so badly I dropped my brush with a loud clang on the floor.

"Here, let me get that for you Eliza," said Simon as he bent down to pick it up.

"Thank you, my dearest, very clumsy of me," I said nervously as he kissed me on the cheek.

I could hardly look him in the eye, surely he would notice something was wrong, but he went about his business as if it were any other night. I could hear John and Antoinette's muffled voices coming from the room across the hall but nothing else. My hands and forehead were damp, my nerves getting the better of me. What was I thinking, letting Amelia go like that, and how can I lie to Simon like this, again. In my heart, I was hoping that somehow a disaster would be averted, but what if something happens to Amelia and Fiona in the darkness alone. I would never forgive myself and I am sure Simon would not either.

I lay in bed next to him listening to the sound of his breathing, straining to hear the slightest noise that might signal to me that Amelia had returned. It seemed like hours had passed but truly it could not have been long as the embers in the grate were still glowing red. Was that the squeak of the floorboard? I slipped quietly out of bed and slowly opened the door in time to see Amelia in her night dress coming up the stairs. She wisely must have changed downstairs in case she encountered her father or brother in the darkness. In the moonlight, we could barely see each other but she stopped for a moment and nodded her head as if to say yes, she had accomplished her mission. I let out a sigh of relief just as Simon turned over in bed.

"Eliza?"

"I am sorry, my dear, I did not mean to wake you. I was getting some water, go back to sleep," I said as I pulled the blanket up around him. I climbed in next to him and tried to close my eyes, but still the sleep would not come. I could only think about what might happen next. I must have finally dozed off because the sun was peering through the curtains when Fiona came in.

"Good morning, ma'am, shall I draw you a bath this morning?" she said, trying to sound nonchalant. I sat up in bed and glared at her.

"Fiona do not pretend to me that this is as any other morning. Is Amelia up?"

"No ma'am, she is still sleeping."

"Did you know Fiona, did you know what she was going to do?"

"I am sorry, ma'am, I should have told you. She came to me right after Mrs. Gage left and asked me to help her. I did not know what else to do," she said remorsefully.

"Never again, Fiona, you must tell me if anything like this ever happens again, do you understand?" I said angrily.

"Yes, ma'am, I understand," she replied with a small curtsey.

"Now go and wake Amelia and then come back to help me dress, we must get downstairs before Simon and John become suspicious.

"John is not here, ma'am, he left very early this morning."

My heart sank as a feeling of complete and utter dread engulfed me, its fingers entwined around my chest and squeezing the very air from my lungs. I struggled to breathe. Whatever is happening, it has begun, and it is all in God's hands now.

Chapter Seven

War Begins

After a quiet couple of days, it seems something has changed, and Simon has been at the town commons all morning. William has been going back and forth to bring word to Amelia and me as we wait impatiently at home. There has been an altercation in Lexington we now know as British troops numbering in the hundreds faced off with some eighty-militia gathered on the town green. There were a few shots fired and some of the militias were killed but there were no British casualties.

"Amelia, stop, you will wear a path in the floorboards," I said as I watched her pacing back and forth nervously, stopping from time to time to peer out through the curtains.

"I am sorry mother," she said as she came and sat beside me.

"Do you know where Nathaniel and Benjamin are?" I asked softly.

"No, of course not, I am not conspiring with them mother, I simply felt … compelled to tell them what I had heard."

I held my finger up to my lips as Antoinette came through the doorway.

"Any more word from William?" she asked as she sat down across from us, her mending in a basket she placed at her feet.

"No, nothing new I am afraid," I said as I watched her. She seemed so calm, as if confident that John would be unharmed. I wish I could feel that same confidence, but it is the fate of three of my sons that knits my brow and twists my stomach, not just a husband. We never speak about the fact that Nathaniel and Benjamin have joined the Patriots, but I am sure it must weigh on her as it must on John as well no matter how much he says to the contrary.

The clock strikes two just as Simon and William come through the door. In the street, I can hear much more commotion and wagons are moving west out of town.

"William, bring the wagon around front, Eliza there has been a battle outside of Concord and there are many dead and wounded. We need supplies to care for the injured," said Simon, his voice flat and lifeless.

I barked out orders as I gathered up my skirts and started for the stairs. "Antoinette, get a few of the old sheets and start tearing them into strips. Amelia, go and tell Fiona, she will know what to prepare, I will get some needles, thread, and some knives."

My heart was racing, dead and wounded … surely they must be on both sides. I dumped out the contents of my sewing basket and then began refilling it with just the things I thought they might need before going through Simon's drawer to retrieve a couple of the best hunting knives that he kept there. By the time I reached the front door, William was already waiting with the wagon.

"Blankets too, Amelia, grab a few blankets," I said as I handed the basket up to William.

Simon came out carrying two muskets and a satchel I assumed was full of powder and musket balls.

"I am coming with you."

"No Eliza, you need to stay here, in case..." he hesitated for a moment. "In case any of the boys come here in need of aid."

"Fiona can handle anything that comes. I am going, my flesh and blood, my very heart may be lying hurt, dying, and I will not sit idly by and do nothing."

"Get in," he said reluctantly.

We joined the sea of wagons headed west toward Concord as word began to filter back through the line. After a minor skirmish in Lexington, the Army had headed to Concord where there was a belief that arms were being stored by the Patriots, but when they arrived, they realized that nearly all of them had been moved. The soldiers decided to burn what was left but the fire quickly got out of control. Perhaps thinking that the British were going to burn down the town, the militia advanced on a contingent of soldiers who were stationed at the North Bridge. The soldiers fired first but the militia returned fire and the troops fell back.

Soon, the entire British column of soldiers was headed back toward Boston when the militia, now grown to several thousand, began to engage them, firing from behind trees and buildings as they marched along the road. A running battle ensued leaving hundreds of British soldiers dead and many more wounded.

"Stop the wagons, stop the wagons," came the repeated shout from ahead.

"Simon, why are we stopping?"

"I do not know. William, hold here," said Simon as he jumped down and ran ahead to see why we were no longer moving. Everyone slowly came to a halt as we impatiently waited for word. It took only a few minutes for Simon to return.

"The British troops have fled being sorely out-numbered by the militia and they are headed this way. We need to get off the road to allow them passage."

"But what of the dead and wounded?" I asked as I felt hot tears welling up in my eyes.

"I doubt they will send anyone back as they are in fear of their very lives. Those who are wounded will have to find a way to help themselves, the dead are at God's mercy now and nothing we can do for them will have any bearing," said Simon reluctantly.

"No, I am not turning back. These men, these soldiers and Patriots, they need help, they need our help," I wailed.

"Eliza, the Patriots are in control of the road that lies ahead, do you really think they will allow us to pass?"

"We can try, perhaps they will turn us away but if we can save even a few, we should give it our best effort."

Simon stood by the side of the wagon looking up at me, his face revealing the torment he must be feeling. I was not the only one wondering if one or more of my sons lay dead on the road ahead.

"William, if you do not want to go forward with us you can return with one of the other wagons," said Simon as he climbed aboard.

"No sir, I will stay with you and Mrs. Parkman if you do not mind."

"Thank you, William, your uncle would be very proud of you," said Simon as he took the reins and maneuvered onto the grass to go around the wagons trying to turn around.

It was not long before we started passing the returning troops, now marching quickly in a haphazard column. We waited patiently on the side of the road while they passed with Simon inquiring of a few men as to where John's regiment might be, but no one seemed to know. In the chaos, all order had broken down and men scattered like leaves in the wind, each concerned about nothing more than their own survival.

Soon we started to find the bodies of British soldiers littering the road. The smell of blood and death permeated the air mixed with smoke from a few smoldering fires. The stench burned my nostrils and choked in my throat as I gulped, trying to breathe.

"Here, put this over your nose and mouth," said William as he handed me his handkerchief dampened with water. "It will help with the smell."

Death is not a stranger to me, to anyone really, we live with it around us all the time. We lose a child, we bury our parents, our siblings, our friends, but I have never seen death on this scale before, even during the pox. Simon and William were now having to move bodies from the road so that we can continue, and I drive the wagon slowly trying to avoid the pools of blood. They carefully turn over each soldier in an officer's uniform to see who it is. *It is not John,* I say to myself each time, and each time I am able to breathe again until we find another body, and then another.

We have found two soldiers badly wounded but alive and they are lifted carefully into the back of the wagon where I can tend to their wounds. This means Simon must now drive the wagon leaving William to the grim task of dragging bodies out of the way alone. With each rut in the road one of the men moans quietly, but the other makes no sound at all. I see a few men in civilian clothes lying dead along the tree line, but William stays on the road fearful of going too close to the trees. As we rounded a corner, we are met by a dozen or so militia who have block-aded the road, several have raised their muskets in our direction.

"Whoa," says Simon pulling up tightly on the reins as the wagon comes to a halt.

"It is not safe for you to be out on this road, turn around now," yelled one of the men.

"Those are redcoats in the back!" said one of the men.

I stood up in the back of the wagon and raised my hands to show them I held no weapon even as William reached over the side of the wagon to grab his gun.

"No William, do not," said Simon quietly.

"I am Mrs. Parkman, this is my husband Simon and our servant William, we are here to help the wounded," I said loudly.

"Ma'am the redcoats do not need your help, you need to go back to Boston, and you need to go now," he said, firmly gesturing the way we had come.

"We are not just here to help the British, we are looking for anyone who may need our help, even those with whom you fight."

"What did you say your name was?" a different man asked as he lowered his musket.

"Mrs. Parkman, Eliza Parkman."

"You are Nathaniel Parkman's mother?" he asked.

"Yes, yes I am, and this is his father, Simon."

The men gathered and spoke in low tones we could not make out as they gestured in our direction. Finally, they began to move the wooden blockade off one side of the road.

"Mrs. Parkman, Nathaniel is up the road aways here and there are several wounded men with him. If you wish to go on, we will give you safe passage," said the man who seemed to be in charge.

Simon nodded and we moved forward again with each of the men nodding at us as we passed. Nathaniel was here alive; I could only hope the same could be said of Benjamin and John. By the time we reached the next blockade it was nearly dark, but they seemed to be expecting us and they quickly moved the barrier and motioned for us to move off the road toward a clearing. There, huddled around a few small fires were twenty or thirty men and a few wounded and dead British soldiers as well as several wounded militia, some men standing guard and others attending to the wounded. Nathaniel seemed to appear out of nowhere as I scrambled out of the wagon to embrace him.

"Mother, once again you are somewhere you do not belong," he said as he held me at arm's length.

"I know, but by now you should realize that wherever my children are is a place I belong, no matter the risk," I said, so relieved to see him.

"Have you seen your brothers?" asked Simon as he tied up the horses to a small tree.

"Benjamin was well behind the fighting and so I am sure he is safe. John stayed with his regiment and was on horseback the last time I saw him. Josiah is dead," he said grimly as he motioned to one of the bodies lying in a row waiting to be buried.

I covered my face with my hands, Josiah was a part of our family, Antoinette's only blood family here, she will be crushed.

"Nathaniel, you did not…"

"No mother I was not involved in the fighting which took Josiah's life. We found him when we moved forward into this field, along with several of his men."

I breathed a sigh of relief; I did not know what I would say to Antoinette had Nathaniel been directly involved in his death.

"Sargent Wood is here; he has been wounded. Mother, would you tend to him? I will help father bury Josiah," said Nathaniel pointing toward the soldier lying quietly near the fire.

I nodded silently as I took my basket from the back of the wagon. The Sergeant's wounds were deep, and he was burning with a fever, mumbling to himself as many of the wounded were. I bandaged him as best I could, but it was clear his wound was most egregious.

"Mother," the Sargent whispered.

"No, it is Mrs. Parkman, you have been wounded."

'Mother, I am sorry," he said, his voice gurgling in his throat.

If it was his mother he needed, it was his mother I would be.

"My son, what would you ever have to be sorry for?" I asked as I wiped the trickle of blood now seeping from the corner of his mouth.

"I promised you I would come home…"

"You are home my dearest boy; you are home do not fear."

He smiled slightly and then he took his last breath and spoke no more.

I could see Simon and Nathaniel digging a grave for Josiah and my heart just broke for him. Josiah was almost like a brother to Simon, and he must be feeling this loss most painfully.

William brought a blanket from the wagon and Simon carefully wrapped Josiah's body in it after removing his insignia and putting it in his pocket. I approached them as they carefully laid his body in the hole they had dug.

"We should say something," said Simon, his voice cracking with emotion as he looked at Nathaniel.

"Dear Lord, we commend to your care the body and soul of our brethren, Josiah Hutton, who has in this life been your faithful and dutiful servant. We ask that you in your most merciful wisdom, take his soul unto heaven to be with you and that you provide your comfort and grace to those he has left behind on this earth who will grieve his passing. In Jesus' name, Amen."

"Amen," I said quietly.

I looked at Nathaniel to see tears slowly trickling down his face, and he wiped them away on his sleeve.

"Thank you, son," said Simon as he began to shovel the dirt, slowly obscuring the white sheet until nothing but dirt could be seen.

We had no choice but to stay the night here as it was unsafe to travel in the dark and I continued to tend to the wounded as the other men continued to dig graves and bury the dead. I finally fell asleep exhausted next to the fire but awoke to find Simon and Nathaniel nearby deep in conversation.

"Father, we have tried over and over again to avoid this bloodshed, but the Crown had no desire to hear our pleas, they have fallen on deaf ears. We want peace, our cause was not to bring death and destruction but to bring equality and liberty to all men," said Nathaniel.

"But now it is war Nathaniel, and men, men like Josiah, like your brother John, like you, will die, and die for what?"

"We will die for our freedom, for our right to be treated fully as men in charge of their own destiny, their own future. If this is not something worth dying for then I do not know what is," he said with sincerity.

"You will raise your musket against your very own brother?"

"It brings me no pleasure, father, I assure you, but we must each live, and die by the strength of our own convictions and by what is in our hearts. I know you do not agree with my choice, with Benjamin's choice, but I hope you can find a way to respect us for doing what we feel is right."

Simon nodded and put his arm around Nathaniel, pulling him close to him and kissing him on the cheek.

"You are my son, you will have my love and respect always, for as you say a man who follows his truth, and his heart cannot be held in contempt by any man."

In the misty morning light, we loaded as many of the wounded as we could into the wagon and said our goodbyes.

"Take care, you and your brother both," said Simon as he embraced Nathaniel.

"I will, father."

I did not know if we would see Nathaniel again, but I was heartened that he and his father had made their peace. We took the rest of the British wounded with us, but the wounded militia stayed behind knowing they would be imprisoned should they go to Boston. Sadly, Sargent Wood died during the night, and we buried him next to Josiah. As the wagon started slowly down the road, I turned to take one last look at Nathaniel before he was swallowed up in the morning mist, disappearing as if he had been an apparition.

By the time we reached Boston, it was clear no one would be going in and out again. The city was surrounded by the Patriots and Governor Gage and his troops had taken refuge along Massachusetts Bay where the docked ships could provide additional firepower.

When we arrived at home, dirty and tired, we were relieved to see John, with several others from his regiment, waiting for us and they joined William on the wagon to take the wounded men to the field hospital. I was desperately in need of a bath but there was something we needed to do first as Simon and I sought out Antoinette who was waiting with Amelia in the parlor.

Simon sat down next to her as she looked at him quizzically.

"What is it, Father?"

Simon reached into his pocket and pulled out Josiah's insignia and placed it in Antoinette's hand curling her fingers around it as he held her hand in his.

"I am sorry Antoinette, Josiah was killed in the fighting," he said gently.

She stared at him as the tears began to well up in her eyes, then suddenly she jerked her hand away from Simon as she stumbled to her feet.

"This," she said struggling to get out her words, "this travesty is because of men like Nathaniel and Benjamin, men who have no respect or loyalty to the country that has made their lives here possible. They are not Patriots. They are vile, treasonous vermin who should all be hanged!" she spat out with a venom that made me cringe. And with that she turned and ran up the stairs wailing the entire way, slamming the bedroom door to punctuate her pain.

Amelia rose to go after her, but I grabbed her hand.

"No dear, let her grieve in her own way, I do not think she wants to talk to any of us at this moment, and perhaps it is for the best."

I finally made my own way upstairs and Fiona helped me undress, piling up my filthy clothes in the corner.

"Burn them," I said without emotion, "I cannot look upon them again without seeing death and despair."

She nodded, trying to hold in her own emotions. Once I was in the warm bath, I scrubbed vigorously on my skin to remove the blood and dirt that had accumulated there, as if in doing so I would wash it from my mind as well. But my mind would not be calmed, and my tears flowed freely. My sobs shook my whole body as I grieved for Antoinette, for the men we have lost, and for men we have still to lose.

Chapter 8

The Siege of Boston

We gathered for dinner that night without Antoinette who decided to take her meal in her room, not able to face us after this morning's outburst. I could certainly not blame her. We ate quietly for the most part, everyone lost in their own thoughts, until John broke the silence.

"They knew we were coming," he said to no one in particular.

Simon put down his knife and fork and looked at John as he wiped his face.

"Why do you say that son?"

"We know from our intelligence that they were stockpiling munitions in that barn in Lexington, but when we arrived the arms had been moved, they had to have known we were coming."

I glanced over at Amelia as she pushed food around her plate with her fork, afraid perhaps to make eye contact with John.

"You cannot know that for certain," replied Simon, "Perhaps it was just a bit of luck on their part."

"I do not know if it was luck or treachery, but Governor Gage insists that very few knew about the plan, even I did not know until Josiah told me the night before we departed."

"Whatever the case it is done, so what is the Governor's plan now that Boston is surrounded by this so-called Continental Army?"

"They are preparing to engage the enemy as soon as an appropriate place for an attack can be determined," said John as he drained his wine glass.

The enemy, the words rang through my head like a gong echoing over and over. John's wrath was directed at the Patriots but unbeknownst to him it was also directed at his sister, and at me. Was Amelia the reason the arms had been moved? We might never know for certain, but the strong possibility certainly existed. I have never felt so uncomfortable in my own skin, and I am sure Amelia was feeling the same.

"How is Antoinette?" I asked finally, trying to change the subject.

"As you would expect," said John. "She has asked me to return her and the children to our home in the morning," he added flatly.

'Surely, John, it is safer for her and the children to stay here," I protested.

"She is not concerned about their safety, mother; we are in control of Boston now. She is, however, no longer comfortable staying here. I can only hope with the passage of time that will change."

I felt the fabric of my family tearing again, now my grandchildren would be taken from my home, and I did not know when I might see them again. This situation seemed to grow worse by the day with no end in sight.

Over the next few weeks, we boarded up the windows in the house and did our best to prepare for anything that might come. The house was quiet now with just the three of us here, although Fiona, Ethan, and William are often staying the night now as the streets are still not safe. The Patriots were squarely in control of the routes in and out and they had effectively cut Boston off from the rest of the colony. The British mostly controlled Boston Harbor but there were still a few ships under the flag of the Continental Army that were harassing British ships and impacting the delivery of arms and goods sorely needed by the troops.

"In a few days, troops will be moving out of Boston to try and fortify some of the hills surrounding the city in order to improve their ability to control the harbor," said Simon as he and I and Amelia sat in the parlor after dinner.

"Surely that will bring this to an end, will it not?" I asked hopefully.

"No, I do not think it will accomplish so lofty a goal, but it will mean that supplies can get in and out of the harbor more easily," he said as he finished his whiskey.

"That will certainly be welcome. Our larders are becoming quite bare and with little access to the fields there's not much hope for the summer harvest," I added.

"Does this mean there will be a fight?" asked Amelia, her voice trembling a bit.

"Hopefully not, Gage thinks he can get there before the Continentals and gain the upper hand so a conflict might yet be avoided," replied Simon as he reached over and patted her hand.

He looked at her the tears starting to well up in her eyes, "You are worried about your brothers?"

"Yes father, are you?"

"Always..." said Simon as he squeezed her hand.

"Eliza, I am going to the warehouse. I want to make sure the building is secure and although there are no barrels of rum left that building is still an important investment we must protect at least for now."

"Now darling? It is almost dark and with the checkpoints and soldiers in the street it will take some time."

"I know but I will not sleep without being sure that it is secure. I may not be back till morning, but William will be here with you."

"Of course, we will be fine, do not worry about us."

The evening passed quietly, and I focused on my needlepoint. Fiona has gone to visit a sick friend nearby and so I wandered into the kitchen to gather some meat, cheese, and bread for Amelia and I for a simple dinner when I noticed a lantern burning in the barn. Ethan had left after seeing Simon off and William was stoking the fire in the parlor. *Perhaps Simon had left it burning*, best to go and put it out to avoid a fire. I took the lantern from the kitchen with me but as I approached the barn the light suddenly went out. I hesitated, *it must have blown out*, but it was a very still evening, no breeze was blowing. The door to the barn opened with a loud creak and I held my lantern up high as I looked around, but I saw nothing but the shadows. Silverstone, in the stall at the far end of the barn, snorted and pawed at the ground, perhaps he was excited thinking he was going out.

"I am sorry my dear boy, but we are not going out this evening," I said as I walked toward him. "Perhaps I should have brought you something from the kitchen," I added as I stroked his muzzle.

He whined and stomped his hoof as though chastising me for my lack of consideration. Suddenly I felt a strong arm around me, holding me tightly with a hand over my mouth. I tried to wiggle free, but it tightened even more as I struggled against its grip.

"Do not scream," said the man's voice in my ear as he loosened his grip and removed his hand from my mouth.

"Benjamin!"

"Not so loud, mother, we do not want to alert William."

"We?"

"Yes mother, we," said Amelia as she came out of the shadows from the stall next to Silverstone.

I looked back and forth between their faces, and I knew at once what was happening.

"Amelia, you are spying on your father, on us!" I cried out feeling the weight of her actions bearing down on me.

"Shh, lower your voice," said Benjamin as he glanced toward the door.

"Mother, I am sorry, I am truly, but I am doing what I feel I must," whispered Amelia.

"Benjamin, this is your fault, you and Nathaniel, you have put your sister and me in a most untenable position, why would you do such a thing?" I asked as I pounded his chest with my fists with an anger I do not think I have ever felt before.

"No, mother stop, it was not them, it was me," said Amelia, now just a few inches from me, her face illuminated in the light. I could see her eyes were bright and in them I also saw something else, a change I had not noticed before, a determination.

"Mother, we would never have asked Amelia to betray you, to betray father," said Benjamin as he held my arms.

"I volunteered, mother. I believe in the cause, and I stand with Benjamin and Nathaniel and all of the others in this fight for our equality and liberty," she said vehemently.

My face was flushed, and I felt as if I were trying to breathe underwater as my knees started to buckle.

"Here, sit down," said Benjamin as he half carried me toward a bale of hay, where I sat trying to collect myself when we heard a noise.

"British troops," whispered Amelia and Benjamin quickly extinguished my lantern.

"Not a sound mother, please."

We could hear the faint drumbeat growing louder as the sound of soldiers marching past the barn filled me with dread, what if we were discovered? We could hear their cadence being called out as they shuffled past just feet away from where I sat. I held my breath, if we were caught, certainly we would all be jailed or worse. The shame of it all would be too much for Simon and John. Benjamin sat next to me and held onto me tightly and I could see he was prepared to clamp his hand over my mouth again should it be necessary, but I had no intention of making a sound. Finally, it was quiet again and we each breathed a sigh of relief.

"Benjamin, how did you get in the city, why are you here?"

"We have a way to go in and out without being discovered. There are those sympathetic to the cause in the city, and we communicate via lantern. When there is important information to be shared, Amelia signals from her window and the message is passed to me. We then meet here in the barn to exchange information."

"I see," I said, still in shock.

"So, you are here because of what Simon said earlier about Gage preparing to move troops to better protect the harbor?"

"Yes mother, that is why Amelia summoned me, and I have to go now, I cannot risk staying any longer and I must pass this on to command, quickly."

I nodded, as I looked into his eyes in the lamplight. I could see the fear, but I could also see the resolve, the conviction of his choice.

"Benjamin, I know you and Nathaniel are doing what you feel is true and right and I will pray for your safety, but please do not come here again," I said reluctantly.

"I understand mother, do not fret. I will not place you and father in harm's way again," he said as he kissed me on the forehead.

"God's speed brother," said Amelia as she embraced Benjamin, and then he was gone, a shadow disappearing into the night.

"Come mother, we need to get back to the house, surely William has realized by now that we are here," she said as she helped me up. I suddenly felt every year of my age and it was all I could do to return to the house and indeed we encountered William who was on his way to the barn.

"Mrs. Parkman is all well?" he asked looking at me intently. I felt like he could see right through me, and I could not find the words to respond.

"No cause for concern William, I had gone out to check on the new mare. I thought I saw her limping yesterday and mother came to get me for dinner," said Amelia, smiling at him.

She lied so easily, it made me wonder how many times she has lied to her father and I of which we were not aware. We sat and ate quietly, not speaking to each other as I continued to relive the events of the last hour. I knew now that I had no choice but to tell Simon what was happening, it was unfair to have him cuckolded in his own home by his own family. I do not know how he will react, but it must be done, there can be no more secrets, not Amelia's and not my own. I admit my heart has been more and more with the Patriots and perhaps, if it were not for Simon, I would have openly supported them, but I cannot see my way clear to betray my husband.

Simon was not born here, he is English through and through, but I am not. This very soil runs through my veins as sure as my blood and this land, this place, these people, we have built a life here for one-hundred-and-fifty-years. We have defined ourselves, our dreams and aspirations are ignited by our surroundings, our neighbors and friends, not by a government in a distant land. We have a right to be treated the same as any other man or woman who resides in the motherland. We should not be told with whom we can trade or who can manage our local affairs, and we certainly should not be taxed to fill the coffers of Parliament.

I looked at Amelia sitting quietly across from me, and I wondered what she would think if she knew how I really felt. But as much as I would like to tell her, I cannot abandon my husband, my vows, even though I agree with what she and the boys are espousing. There is also the matter of John, who feels so ardently, even more so than his father perhaps, that these demands are treason of the highest order, and that any resistance must be quashed. I do not know what has driven this fervor in him, perhaps it is Antoinette or the influence of Josiah, but even if Simon's position is not so intractable, John's most certainly is. How could I possibly choose some of my children over the others? I have tried my very best to stay neutral in this debate but, in reality, I have never been and now I must face that too no matter what happens next.

Simon did not return in the morning and by midday my concern could be contained no longer.

"William, have you heard from Master Simon? I am starting to worry."

"No Ma'am I have not, and I share your concern. With your permission, I will ride over to the warehouse to see if he is there, if not perhaps I can determine where he has gone."

"Of course, William, thank you."

I set about helping Fiona with the washing to keep my mind occupied, but it was less than an hour before William returned to the house, barreling through the back door.

"Mrs. Parkman, Fiona!" he called out frantically.

"Here William, we are here, what is it?" I called out.

"Master Simon, he has fallen from a ladder at the warehouse, he has broken his leg and needs our help," he said breathlessly.

"William, calm yourself, get the wagon and bring it out front. Fiona and I will gather up some things we will require. But we will also need some help to get him in the wagon. See if Eli is next door, he is the son of Mrs. Keene and he can help us lift him."

In just a few minutes, the four of us were going at full speed to the warehouse, only to be stopped by a checkpoint just a short distance from our destination.

"Halt, stop!" demanded the soldier at the checkpoint. I should have anticipated this, an empty wagon moving quickly near the wharf was bound to be a source of concern.

"I am Mrs. Simon Parkman," I replied quickly, "My husband has been injured at our warehouse and we are going to his aid. Please we need to get through," I said pleading with the sentry.

"Proceed," said the guard as he and the other soldiers stepped aside, and we hurried on toward the wharf. Once my eyes had adjusted to the dim light inside it was easy to find Simon sprawled out on the floor underneath one of the windows. The ladder lay by his side broken into several pieces, as was his leg which was bent at a most unnatural angle. He moaned quietly but did not speak although he was able to sip a bit of the water I gave him.

"Eli, break the ladder apart more and find me two pieces of about the same size and length. We need to make a splint before we try to put Simon in the wagon."

We set to work creating the splint as Fiona tore a sheet into strips we could use to tie the boards onto Simon's leg. Now was the difficult part.

"William, Eli, do either of you have a flask?"

"I do Mrs. Parkman," said Eli as he pulled the silver bottle from his jacket pocket.

"Simon, here you need to drink this, as much as you can," I said as I lifted his head up and laid it in my lap. Slowly he sipped at the flask, and I kept pouring until it was empty.

"William, bring the wagon inside as close to here as you can. Fiona, help me roll Simon onto the blanket."

With each movement, Simon moaned quietly but his eyes remained closed. Now the hard part, to put on the splint. It took all four of us and Simon screamed in pain, but we could not stop, we had to keep going. Finally, we were ready. We each grabbed a corner of the blanket, the men in the front, and we lifted Simon up to the back of the wagon. His cries became a bit louder but stopped as soon as we laid him down once again. I am sure the jostling was quite painful but the worst of it was over at least for now, and the whiskey was helping to ease his torment.

Fiona and I did our best to keep Simon still as we bumped along the roads and, thankfully, the check-point did not delay us on our return trip. We stopped long enough to let Fiona out at Doctor Snow's house so that she could tell him what had happened. Amelia had gathered a few more of the men from surround-ing homes so when we arrived there was plenty of help to transport Simon up the stairs to our room for which I was most grateful.

"How bad is it, mother?" asked Amelia shakily.

"His leg is broken quite badly, and he is bruised and battered but I am hopeful Doctor Snow can help him heal, for now we need to pray."

"I have sent word to John," said Amelia.

"Just John?"

Amelia looked at me thoughtfully, "Yes mother, just John but if you think I should, I can try to get a message through to…"

She did not have to say it, and I nodded my approval. I did not know how bad things were, but Nathaniel and Benjamin should know at least that their father had been injured. Hours passed before the Doctor joined us in the parlor.

"Mrs. Parkman, I have done all I can for now. I will return in the morning to check on your husband."

"Thank you, Doctor Snow, is his leg going to heal?"

He shrugged his shoulders and gestured toward the sky, "It is in God's hands now, we will have to wait and see. He may keep the leg yet, but time will tell."

I recoiled at his words as the gravity of Simon's injuries was now apparent.

"He could lose his leg?"

"Yes, I do not know if it will heal properly or at all and if it does not, we will have to amputate most likely to avoid disease," he said solemnly as he tipped his hat on the way out the door.

I spent the rest of the afternoon at Simon's bedside, but he never stirred. The Doctor had given him some laudanum and he was sleeping soundly. His leg was still splinted but now straight and heavily bandaged. Now in the light I could see various cuts and bruises on his face and arms, and his left hand was also splinted and bandaged, an injury I had not noticed before.

John arrived that evening looking quite flustered but not just because of his father it turned out. After sitting with him for a few minutes, we moved to the parlor so as not to disturb Simon. Fiona would stay with him for a while. I filled John in on all the Doctor had said, but it was clear he had bigger concerns.

"What is it John, I can see you are deeply distressed, know we are doing everything we can for your father, and I pray God will grant his grace and healing. We can do little more."

"I know mother, I trust Doctor Snow and I am sorry I could not be here earlier to help you. I am sure father will be well, but there is a battle brewing, and tomorrow will be difficult."

"A battle?" asked Amelia.

"Yes, over the last few nights a significant number of colonial troops have taken up positions on Bunker and Breed's Hill and constructed a redoubt as well as fortified lines across the Charlestown Peninsula. This now gives them better control over the harbor and a defensible position our cannons cannot reach."

"But I thought Governor Gage was going to occupy those hills. Simon mentioned it just a couple of days ago," I said with surprise.

"Exactly, once again they seem to know our plan of attack and they have beaten us to the punch," he said with exasperation.

I looked at Amelia who met my gaze without so much as a blink, this time I've no doubt that what she told Benjamin was the source of the Colonial Army's information.

"We will attack at first light," added John.

My heart and mind were overwhelmed. My husband is lying upstairs gravely injured, and now my sons will meet on the battlefield tomorrow. I could not know how this fight would end but I did know for certain that one or more of my sons would be on the losing side.

The battle lasted for days, with two major British assaults repulsed by the Patriots, and many British casualties, but Gage persisted and finally captured their positions on the third assault after the Colonial Army ran out of ammunition. The colonists retreated over the hill leaving the British in control but not before General Warren, known before as Doctor Warren was killed, along with many, many others including many British officers.

John received only a minor flesh wound thankfully and Amelia was able to get word from Benjamin that he and Nathaniel had also survived and they were holed up on the outskirts of town. The British seemed to have won the battle, but we were still at war with Boston more and more isolated, and the basics of life were harder and harder to come by. Amidst all this anguish, heartache and death, Simon continued to sleep, oblivious to it all.

Chapter Nine

Retreat

Simon sits quietly by the fire in our room drinking weak tea and broth as he pulls his blanket up around his shoulders. His recovery has been slow and while his leg has healed a great deal these past many months, he is still barely able to get up and down the stairs and spends most of his days in our room, reading and sleeping. He keeps up with his newspapers and visits regularly with John to keep up with what is happening, which is to say little. We continue to be isolated from the rest of the colony, but at least no further large-scale entanglements have occurred, just constant skirmishes between the Continental soldiers and the British along the perimeter.

Benjamin was able to get some supplies in to us for which I am most grateful, but I dare not tell his father from where our blessings have come for fear he might mention it to John. He does not remember his fall and often has trouble recalling things he is very familiar with. He is here with us, but not fully in the way he was before, and he talks little unless prompted. I have also not told him about Amelia for the same reason, and perhaps it would be more than he can bear in his current state.

The winter thaw has begun, and I try to get Simon to take some fresh air, but he has little interest and I abandon my efforts quickly. No matter, after a few nice days it has turned windy and cold again with a hard rain. The city is grey and overcast, matching the mood of its inhabitants as if we were one with the sky, foreboding and melancholy. I fear Amelia's youth is wasting away with no social events and she no longer takes the calls of any potential suitors. She still tutors a young lady in French and another in prose, but most are too preoccupied with securing necessaries for survival to worry about furthering their education.

John comes to the house nearly daily, but we have not seen Antoinette or the children since Josiah died over a year ago. John speaks to me of them and I can only hope that he tells the children how much we love and miss them. It is out of my control and Antoinette's wishes as their mother must be respected. Perhaps when this is all over, we will be united as a family again, but I do not know if forgiveness can be found in her heart.

I awoke early this morning to the sound of distant cannon fire reverberating through the air and when I looked out the window, I could see the smoke rising in the distance. I dressed quickly but did not find William in the house so I decided to set off on my own to the Commons to see what I could discover. There were many gathered there but no one seemed to know what was happening and we all milled about helplessly waiting to see if someone in the British command would speak to us. As it happens, that someone was the newly-promoted Major John Parkman, who climbed the steps of the Commons to survey the crowd.

"Citizens of Boston, you have no cause for concern. The enemy is simply harassing us with their cannon fire, causing no real damage. Please, return to your homes, you are not in danger," said John loudly as the people congregated at his feet.

"Why are you not attacking them?" yelled a man standing just behind me.

"Yes, why? We cannot take much more of this siege," yelled another.

John raised his hands to calm the crowd, "Citizens, please calm yourselves, we are not unsympathetic to your trials, and we are fully engaged with the enemy at every opportunity."

"Tory vermin!" shouted a woman to my left just before a rotten apple, thrown by someone to his right, hit John squarely in the chest. In an instant, the soldiers that had been standing quietly nearby leaped into action, grabbing and dragging away the perpetrator. The remaining soldiers then formed a line at the bottom of the stairs and began slowly pushing the crowd back.

"You are ordered to disperse," yelled John over the line of soldiers. "Go back to your homes at once."

The soldiers kept moving slowly but persistently as the crowd compressed more and more and people began jostling each other as they tried to get away from the moving crowd. I could feel the pressure of the bodies closing in on me and people began shouting for others to move to avoid being trampled. I tried to get out of the way, but someone was standing on the edge of my cloak, and I was frozen in place. Before I knew it, I had toppled to the ground and bodies began falling on top of me, crushing me with their weight as I screamed for help. Suddenly, I felt someone pushing people off of me as another man grabbed me and pulled me up from the ground, gathering me in his arms like a child. My chest hurt, my face burned, and I could feel a trickle of blood oozing down the side of my face.

I did not know who the man was, but he was strong and forceful as he pushed his way out of the crowd with help from the other man who had first saved me. As I clung to him, I could hear people screaming for help all around us before the world closed in and then went dark.

When I awoke there was a cool cloth on my head, and I was lying on a small bed in a modest room, but I could not say where. My head pounded and my stomach churned, my body felt as if I had been caned from head to toe. I tried to sit up.

"No Ma'am, I think you should just lie still a bit more and git your bearings a bit before ye try and git up," said a woman coming out from the shadows. Her accent was a bit Irish but also a bit Scottish, in its tone. She was a very buxom woman in a simple dress and apron with her hair piled on top her head but at the same time eschewed with strands going off in every direction. Her hands were rough and red as she plumped the pillow behind me. I lie back down, and she takes the cloth from my head, rinsing it in the bedside basin and putting it back on my forehead. She gives me a mug of ale and while the taste was abhorrent the liquid felt good on my parched throat.

"Who are you?" I asked finally.

"I am Mrs. Ayers," she said with a mostly toothless grin.

"I am Mrs…"

"I know who ya are," she replied before I could finish.

Just then the door opened and the man who had carried me away from the crowd came into the room. I could see into the room behind him, and it appeared to be a tavern of some sort and there were a few men sitting at tables.

"Aye yar awake!" said the man in an even heavier accent than the woman.

"I am, I want to thank you, sir, for helping me," I said as Mrs. Ayers helped me sit on the side of the bed.

"I taint no sir, but you can call me Hamish, Hamish Ayers, ma'am."

"Thank you, Mr. Ayers, Hamish, I do not know what I would have done without your help, and the other man who was with you."

"A mighty gruesome sight it was, a few people were killed and many a more were a hurt," he said, shaking his head. I could not believe what I was hearing. I might have been killed if Hamish had not saved me.

"Why, Hamish, why did you help me and not someone else?" I asked, the tears welling up behind my eyes.

"Well ma'am, let me say twas not just me luck that brought me to your side this m'rning but as Nathaniel had asked me to keep my eye on you, I do my best," he said smiling, with even less teeth than his wife.

"What do you mean Nathaniel asked you?" I said in disbelief.

"Some time ago, young Nathaniel spoke to me. I am told when you or Amelia leave your house and my job is to make sure ya both return safely."

"But how do you know when I leave?"

"Fiona, she gets a message to me and tells me where ya are headed, but today, I did not know in time, I am sorry ma'am."

Just then, the door opened and a young man I recognized joined us. It was Eli Keene from next door. I could see now that he was the man who had first helped me.

"Mrs. Parkman, I am most heartened to see you sitting there," he said, his hat in his hand.

"Eli, Fiona tells you, doesn't she?"

"Yes ma'am, she does, sometimes Amelia, but mostly Fiona, but today you left the house before she arrived and before Amelia was up, so we had to work together to figure out where you had gone."

I sat there dumbfounded by what I was being told. Fiona had been in league with Amelia after all and her contriteness was just a front to avoid being discovered. Apparently, after Simon was hurt, Nathaniel had asked his fellow Sons of Liberty patriots to keep an eye on us to ensure our safety.

"But why, Eli, Hamish, why would you do this, I am not an open supporter of your cause, why would you help me? I understand Amelia but why, why me?"

Eli pulled up a rickety wooden chair, set it alongside the bed and sat down on it next to me.

"Nathaniel and Benjamin are important leaders in this fight, if they are distracted worrying about your safety they cannot focus on the battles ahead, and so those of us who are here, trapped in Boston, we do what we can to support those who cannot be here themselves. We know you must remain loyal to your husband, but I also know you have supported your sons in your own way, and so it is that we support you," Eli said sincerely.

"Thank you, all of you most truly, but I must be getting home. Amelia must be worried, and Simon will wonder why I have not come to him."

"We sent word to Amelia, not to worry she and Fiona are looking after Mr. Parkman."

Mrs. Ayers helped me to my feet, and I embraced her and each one in turn before Eli helped me to slip out the back door of the tavern and onto the street. I could still hear the cannons firing in the distance as we walked the short distance back to the house.

"Thank you, Eli, thank you for everything and please if you can, send my love and thanks to Nathaniel and Benjamin."

"I will Mrs. Parkman," he said with a nod of his head.

"And Eli, be careful," I said before turning to go inside.

The door had no sooner closed than Fiona and Amelia came down the stairs.

"Mother, I am so glad you are home, here come lie down in my room," she said as she guided me carefully up the stairs.

"I will fetch some broth," said Fiona as she headed for the kitchen.

"Let me look in on your father first," I said but I need not have worried. Simon was sleeping and seemed not to have been aware that I was even gone.

As I settled into Amelia's bed, Fiona returned with the broth.

"Stay Fiona, I want to … I want to talk to the both of you," I said.

Fiona looked down sheepishly. I am sure she was expecting me to chastise her, but she never could have expected what came next.

"I am grateful to both of you for your unseen care these many months since Simon was hurt and I want you to know I am most appreciative. Fiona, you have always been most dedicated to our family and now that I know what you have been doing for us, I want you to know how much I value you and your friendship to me and, most especially, to Amelia."

The two women looked at each other rather incredulously.

"You are not angry, ma'am?

"No Fiona, I am not angry," I replied.

"Mother, what are you trying to say?"

"My heart and soul have always been with you, with the cause that you and the others fight for liberty and equality and self-determination. It is as much my desire as it is yours, and had it not been for your father and John, I would have been a most ardent supporter. But I could not break my vow to your father. As my husband, I owe him my fealty and I did not want to drive a wedge between my children by openly choosing sides. But know that in my heart of hearts I am with you," I said finally.

Amelia embraced me for a long time, and I held her close to me as Fiona watched with tears in her eyes.

"Now I need to rest, so leave me, and Amelia, please be watchful of your father."

"I will, you need not worry," she said kissing me on the forehead before I laid back and drifted off to a restful slumber.

During the night, the world changed in ways none could have anticipated. Major General John Thomas, under orders from General Washington, secretly overtook the area of Dorchester Heights to the south of the city and began fortifying the hill. The cannons that had been firing for the last couple of days were simply to distract from the noise of the building taking place in another part of Boston. Now there were a dozen cannons that the Continental Army had seized when they took Fort Ticonderoga aimed at the town and harbor. British General Howe had been aware of their efforts and tried to use British ships to attack but the bad weather that had set in made that impossible. Now the British were out-gunned, and the Continental Army was in control.

Four days later, Simon managed to come down-stairs to meet with John who had asked to speak with all of us together, including William and Fiona, which I thought was rather odd. As we each settled into a chair in the parlor, John stood by the window looking out to the street.

"I have always loved this house," he said wist-fully. "I always thought someday my own children might live here."

"John, what is it?" I asked anxiously.

"We, the British Army high command I mean, have determined that staying in Boston is no longer tenable, we cannot defend or hold the city any longer and we have negotiated with General Washington's troops safe passage for our soldiers and for any loyalists who wish to join us."

We all stared at him blankly, unable to comprehend what he was saying but, surprisingly, it was Simon who spoke first.

"You are abandoning Boston?" he asked haltingly.

"Reluctantly, yes father, we have no choice. If we try to fight the results would be catastrophic and we would not be able to recover. We are most fortunate the enemy is permitting us to leave. We are retreating to Nova Scotia where we will regroup."

"So, you are simply going to walk away from your home, from your life here?" I asked skeptically.

"We are, mother, and I am assuming the rest of the family will as well. Of course, William and Fiona, you are welcome to join us. You are like part of the family, and you have been loyal servants now for many years."

"Thank you, Master John," replied William, "I go where Master Simon goes."

"I will stay here," said Fiona quietly.

"You are welcome to stay in the house I am sure," said John curtly. "Mother, Amelia, you need to be ready to go by the day after tomorrow. You will be limited to what you can bring with you so choose those most valuable of items that can generate monies with which to secure new housing and necessities."

"John, you cannot be saying we are to pack up and walk away from our home, from everything we have worked so hard for here?"

"It is exactly what I am saying mother, there is no other choice."

"If I want to go to England, can that be … arranged?" asked Simon quietly.

"Yes father, we can put you on a ship to England if that is what you would prefer. Not everyone will have that option, but I will be sure that you do."

"That is what I wish," he said firmly.

I got up and walked around the room looking at all the precious objects that filled it. I gave birth to my children in this house, my oldest son is buried not far from here as are my parents and my sister. My brothers and their families live not far from here. I could not just leave this place, could I?

"John, there must be another way?"

"Mother, if you and the rest of the family stay, I cannot say how you will be treated when the offending army moves in to take control. You and father have been loyal to the Crown and that will not be taken well, I would fear for your safety, the safety of all of you," he said calmly but firmly.

Amelia had said nothing. She just looked at her hands in her lap as if by some magic the answer would be found. But I already knew what that answer would be.

"I am not leaving," she said at last. "My brothers will not take vengeance on me or this house."

John stared at her in disbelief, and I could see an anger was boiling up in him, an anger that was about to explode.

"It was you, was it not? Deny it!" He spat at Amelia as he raised his hand to strike her, but Simon was able to intervene.

"No son!" he said with all his might as he grabbed John's wrist.

"It was me," said Amelia as she stood her ground, "And I would do it again and again," she said defiantly.

Before John could respond, Simon collapsed on the floor at our feet, the effort too much for him to bear. William and John helped him upstairs and settled him into our bed once more.

"Mother, see that you, father, and William are at the wharf early the day after tomorrow," he said as he left the house, slamming the door behind him.

That night I sat quietly with Simon, neither of us speaking, each deep in our own thoughts. I could see these events have exhausted him and he looked more drawn than I had ever seen him.

"Eliza, my love, I want to die in England," he said softly.

"My darling you are not dying, you just need more time, more time to grow strong again," I said tearfully.

"No, I am dying and now I have a chance to be buried in England with my father and mother, in my homeland."

I took both his hands in mine, looking into his eyes which were now hazy with age, and I knew he was right. As much as I wanted to deny his words I could not, he has been dying before my very eyes for months now and it would soon come to an end.

"We will get you to England, William and I, we will get you home," I said as I laid my head on his shoulder.

"No, my darling, you will not, you need to stay here."

"Simon, I do not understand, what are you saying?"

"You have loved me beyond measure, and I have no doubt you would see me to my end, but you love something else just as much and I cannot ask you to give it up for me when I have so little time left."

"I would do anything for you, you are my husband," I said, not able to hide the anguish I was feeling.

"I know, but I cannot allow it. This is your home, the land of your birth, the place…" he paused for a moment, his body racked by spasms of coughing which he could hardly control. "The place your great-grandmother carved out for you and your family. You belong here, not with me. I belong to another world, but this, this is your place, this is your life."

We said nothing more that night, but I continued for the next two days packing up the things we would need. Despite what Simon had said I could not help but feel it was my duty to be with him, to see him safely to England. Perhaps I could come back after the war was over. As I walked through the house, choosing the few things I would take with me, each memory came flooding back to me and filled my heart and mind with the love that had surrounded me in this place. Amelia said little to me, but I often found her crying when she thought I would not see.

William had loaded up the back of the carriage and Eli came with us so that he could return the carriage to the house. We said our goodbyes on the front porch to Amelia and Fiona. I knew I did not need to worry about them. I am sure Benjamin and Nathaniel will be along when they can and they will take good care of Amelia but still, the parting was most sorrowful.

"Take care my darling daughter and write me as you can, we will be at the Parkman Estate in London staying with your father's nephew David."

"I will mother..." she said as she kissed me on each cheek.

With that we were gone, weaving our way through the throngs of people all headed east to the wharf. Most of the soldiers had left already, leaving just a few behind to guard the wharf. But the Continentals had stayed behind the line and had promised to make no incursions by land until the last soldier had departed but they had harassed some of the ships sailing north. As we pulled up to the wharf, I could see a few people that we knew but many more were staying behind than I had imagined. My brother, James, had died a few months ago but his widow and children were staying as was my brother, Stephen, and his family.

As we waited by the dock for our turn to board, I realized I did not see my bags. I looked all around but they were nowhere to be found.

"William, my bags, I do not see them, we cannot go without my bags, where are they?"

"I told him to put them back," said Simon.

"Simon, why would you do that?" I asked reproachfully.

"Because you are not going, you are staying here," he replied calmly.

I could only shake my head as the tears began to flow.

"You belong here, this is your home and I do not want you in England alone when our children here need you. Nathaniel and Benjamin are right, there are times when men, and women, must fight to throw off the shackles of tyranny that threaten to destroy the lives they deserve to live."

I could not believe what I was hearing and all I could do was hold him close to me in a final embrace.

"I love you Simon, with all my heart. There will never be another and I will be true to you for as long as I live," I whispered in his ear.

"Eliza, I could not have asked for a better wife, a better mother to our children, I will see you again if God extends to us his mercy. Now go home before I change my mind, Amelia is expecting you. Fight Eliza, fight for what is right, and give my love to Nathaniel and Benjamin. My only sorrow in life is that I did not get to see them again," he said as he kissed me goodbye.

I watched as William helped him up the gang-plank. He looked so frail and feeble. I prayed he would survive the journey to die in England as he wished. Eli was kind enough to wait for me as I could not tear myself away even after the ship had made it to the horizon and dipped beyond my view. Within my soul, I felt a sorrow as I had when Simon William was killed, an emptiness that felt like it might overtake me. But I also felt something else. I felt a power, a courage, and yes, some anger that I did not know I possessed. I would join my children in this fight, the fight for this land, for my family, for our right to control our own destiny. We might have taken back Boston, but there was much more to be done.

Chapter Ten

We Declare

It took two days before the Continental Army marched into Boston, General George Washington in the lead with Nathaniel and Benjamin not far behind. People lined the streets and cheered the victors although it was clear there were still some loyalists in the city who had chosen not to leave. It was a joyous moment, and of great relief were the supplies they also brought with them. Amelia, Fiona, and I waited expectantly on the front porch for a couple of hours until, at last, Nathaniel and Benjamin rode up.

They were both dirty and unshaven and thinner than I remembered either of them ever being, but I was beyond grateful and relieved to embrace them both in turn.

"Mother, I am so happy to see you," said Nathaniel as he nearly lifted me off my feet.

"Where is Father?" asked Benjamin.

My heart sank, of course they would not have known that he had sailed and was gone. I could hardly bring myself to tell them.

"Your father did not stay. I am sorry to say he is dying, and he wanted to die in England. John was able to get him and William on a boat which left two days ago. He wanted me to give you both his love and he left a letter for you which Amelia helped him write before he left."

"You chose to stay behind then?" asked Nathaniel with surprise.

"No, I decided to go with your father, but at the final moment he insisted I stay. He knew in my heart that this is where I belong, and he wanted me to be here to help you."

"Help us?" asked Benjamin looking puzzled.

"He believed in what you are doing in the fight. I do not know if this is something he came to late or if it was always in his heart, but he felt he could not betray his country, and I have no doubt he was sincere in his desire for me to stay and join you."

Nathaniel began to weep. I was not sure if they were tears of joy or sorrow, perhaps a bit of both, but we wept, all of us. It was a modest dinner we sat down to that evening, but it was a welcome sight to see Benjamin and Nathaniel at this table again. We had much to talk about, and it was well into the night before we finally went upstairs and fell into bed. It was strange being here without Simon, knowing he would not be coming back, but there were a few of his things still in the room and I would cherish each of them and hold them close. The small portrait I had of him I moved to my bedside table so I could gaze on it each night before I slept and each morning when I awoke. He would always be in my thoughts and in my heart, of that I was most sure.

Sadly, Nathaniel would not be staying long. He wanted to get to Philadelphia to join John Adams and his work with the Continental Congress. He exchanged his horse for a fresh one but was gone again after just a few days. Benjamin would stay for a bit and help the Continental Army set up here in

Boston. They were not concerned that the British would return by land, but our harbor was still a temptation for landing troops or for smuggling supplies. I was grateful to have him stay.

"Benjamin, what do you need, how can your sister and I help," I asked as we finished our morning meal.

"Uniforms, shoes, weapons, and gunpowder," he replied without hesitation.

"Well Amelia, I think we can do something about the first two items on the list," I said optimistically, and she nodded in agreement.

"That would be most helpful mother, it is warm now, but winter will be back upon us before long and many of the militia came to us with nothing but the clothes on their backs and for many that will not be enough. Also, mother, I wanted to ask you about the warehouse, do you still have it."

"Well yes, part of it, your father sold off the north warehouse some time ago, but he kept the one at the wharf. He was there boarding up the windows when he…" my voice trailed off. I could barely think about it even these many months later and the picture in my mind of him lying on the floor is one I wish to erase.

"Of course, Amelia told me what happened. I am sorry, mother, that we couldn't be here for you, for him," he said woefully.

"Do not dwell on it, Benjamin, the warehouse is yours if you need it," I said reassuringly.

"Thank you, mother, we would like to use it for storing munitions we will be off loading at the harbor, and I would like to use it as a place to set up a gunsmithing operation. I have, by necessity, become rather skilled at it," he said smiling.

"Your father would be very proud."

Amelia and I set to turning the parlor into a cutting and sewing room and we enlisted the help of Mrs. Ayers, her niece Mary, Mrs. Keene, her daughter Cynthia, Fiona and her friend Martha, and Mrs. Brown from across the street. Each day, the nine of us would meet to cut and sew uniforms, churning them out as fast as we could and distributing them at the warehouse to those most in need. But soon, it was clear we were running out of material.

"There must be some way to find more cloth, I have no more blankets to offer," said Mrs. Keene with exasperation.

"I have an idea," said Amelia, "But mother, I do not think you are going to be in favor of it."

"My dear, in these circumstances we must do things we might not otherwise do, so what is your idea?"

"There are many abandoned homes vacated by those who have left and while I know the Continentals are using some of them there are many still untouched. Surely they must have left behind clothes, shoes, and bedding that we could use for material?" she said expectantly.

"Now yer thinkin!" chimed in Mrs. Ayers.

"Really?" said Mary, "That seems so vulgar."

I had been thinking the same thing. It would be such a violation to go into the homes of others, some who I considered friends, and help ourselves to their belongings.

"What would be vulgar is our men dying in the cold without warm coats and shoes on their feet," said Martha.

"Yes, you are right Martha, I think perhaps we must set aside our trepidation and make use of what we can. I doubt many of those who have left ever expect to return to what they have left behind and it might as well be put to good use," I said.

"We might even find guns and powder!" added Fiona.

So it was agreed. Fiona and Cynthia hitched up the wagon and we started just two doors down with the home of the Barkwoods who had fled to Nova Scotia. I had been in their home before, but it was eerily quiet, dark, and dusty even though they had only been gone a few months.

"Cynthia and Fiona take the upstairs; you know what we are seeking. Amelia, Mary, and I will take this floor."

We tiptoed around at first like thieves in fear of getting caught but by the time we were finished, we were no longer afraid or ashamed. A pile of blankets, clothes, some that would be made into uniforms and others that could be worn as is, shoes and gloves, but better yet, iron plate that could be melted down into musket balls, and even two muskets!

It took several trips, but we loaded everything into the wagon and Amelia and I drove it down to the warehouse while the others started on the next home a few doors down. Benjamin seemed glad to see us but surprised.

"What are you two doing here?" he asked, wiping the black soot from his hands.

"We have some things for you in the wagon," I said as I led him outside.

"What in the bloody hell!" he exclaimed when he saw the mound covered with a blanket.

"Benjamin!"

"My apologies mother," he said sheepishly. "Where did you get all these things?"

"We helped ourselves to those things left behind by those who will no longer be needing them," said Amelia smiling.

"You did what?" he replied with surprise.

"Benjamin, we did what we thought was right and we have much to show for it, clothes you can use now, material for us to make uniforms, shoes, and look, two muskets and lots of iron to melt down for musket balls," I said as I pulled back the blanket.

Benjamin threw back his head and let out a hearty laugh which was infectious and soon we were all laughing.

"My mother and sister pillaging the homes of Boston."

"Well, my dear brother, when you say it that way it sounds very reprehensible."

"No, my dearest Amelia, it is not. It is indeed a most welcome sight. Is there more?"

"Yes, this was just from one house," I replied smiling, and with that we broke out in peals of laughter again. Although I was laughing it was in part a nervous laugh, I did feel a pang of guilt for taking that which did not belong to us, for violating the sanctity of others' homes. But desperation drives people to do things they might not otherwise do, and I could only hope we would not be judged harshly for it in our final days.

We emptied out the contents of two more homes over the next few days and that gave us more than enough material to sew for many more weeks, churning out dozens of new uniforms. We busily sewed each and every day till our fingers were raw and bloodied.

Word arrived from England this week, a letter from William informing us that Simon had passed away peacefully in his sleep just a few weeks after arriving in London. As he wished, he was buried next to his mother and father, and I could take comfort now in knowing he was at peace.

As we sat this hot July day sewing as always, we began to hear church bells ringing in the distance and in just a few minutes it seemed Benjamin was at the window shouting, "Come mother, Amelia, everyone come, we need to go to the Commons."

We dropped our sewing and scurried out the door, not sure what was the source of his excitement.

"Benjamin, what is it?"

"News from the Continental Congress, they are going to be reading it out in the Commons, we need to hurry."

Indeed, when we reached the Commons, people were streaming in from every direction, men, women, and children, mostly on foot to make room for as many as possible. We pushed as close to the front as we could, and my heart raced a bit remembering the last time I had been at these steps. A man

I did not recognize stood there, a large scroll in his hands as he waited for the crowd to quiet. Finally, he began, his voice ringing out loud and clear.

The unanimous Declaration of the thirteen united States of America, When in the Course of human events, it becomes necessary for one people to dissolve the political bands which have connected them with another, and to assume among the powers of the earth, the separate and equal station to which the Laws of Nature and of Nature's God entitle them, a decent respect to the opinions of mankind requires that they should declare the causes which impel them to the separation.

We hold these truths to be self-evident, that all men are created equal, that they are endowed by their Creator with certain unalienable Rights, that among these are Life, Liberty, and the pursuit of Happiness.

The crowd erupted with cheers and shouts of "hear, hear!" and "Amen!" but he was far from finished.

That to secure these rights, Governments are instituted among Men, deriving their just powers from the consent of the governed.

That whenever any Form of Government becomes destructive of these ends, it is the Right of the People to alter or to abolish it, and to institute new Government, laying its foundation on such principles and organizing its powers in such form, as to them shall seem most likely to affect their Safety and Happiness. Prudence, indeed, will dictate that Governments long established should not be changed for light and transient causes; and accordingly, all experience hath shewn, that mankind are more disposed to suffer, while evils are sufferable, than to right themselves by abolishing the forms to which they are accustomed. But when a long train of abuses and usurpations, pursuing invariably the same Object evinces a design to reduce them under absolute Despotism, it is their right, it is their duty, to throw off such Government, and to provide new Guards for their future security.--Such has been the patient sufferance of these Colonies; and such is now the necessity which constrains them to alter their former Systems of Government. The history of the present King of Great Britain is a history of repeated injuries and usurpations, all having in direct object the establishment of an absolute Tyranny over these States. To prove this, let Facts be submitted to a candid world.

With that, he proceeded to list all the acts committed against the colonies that the Congress had determined were the justification for this declaration. When he reached the *for imposing Taxes on us without our Consent* the crowd broke into cheers again and chants of "no taxation without representation," rang out across the square and continued for many minutes before calm was restored and he continued. It was most shocking how many grievances had been amassed. Finally, the crux of the matter was revealed…

In every stage of these Oppressions, we have Petitioned for Redress in the most humble terms: Our repeated Petitions have been answered only by repeated injury. A Prince whose character is thus marked by every act which may define a Tyrant, is unfit to be the ruler of a free people.

Nor have We been wanting in attentions to our British brethren. We have warned them from time to time of attempts by their legislature to extend an unwarrantable jurisdiction over us. We have reminded them of the circumstances of our emigration and settlement here. We have appealed to their native justice and magnanimity, and we have conjured them by the ties of our common kin-

dred to disavow these usurpations, which would inevitably interrupt our connections and correspondence. They too have been deaf to the voice of justice and of consanguinity. We must, therefore, acquiesce in the necessity, which denounces our Separation, and hold them, as we hold the rest of mankind, Enemies in War, in Peace Friends.

We, therefore, the Representatives of the united States of America, in General Congress, Assembled, appealing to the Supreme Judge of the world for the rectitude of our intentions, do, in the Name, and by Authority of the good People of these Colonies, solemnly publish and declare, That these United Colonies are, and of Right ought to be Free and Independent States; that they are Absolved from all Allegiance to the British Crown, and that all political connection between them and the State of Great Britain, is and ought to be totally dissolved; and that as Free and Independent States, they have full Power to levy War, conclude Peace, contract Alliances, establish Commerce, and to do all other Acts and Things which Independent States may of right do. And for the support of this Declaration, with a firm reliance on the protection of divine Providence, we mutually pledge to each other our Lives, our Fortunes, and our sacred Honor.

The crowd was silent for a few seconds before erupting in joyous cheers and shouting which I am sure could be heard all the way back to London. I embraced my children, my friends, for this was truly what we had hoped for. The reveling went on for hours, the taverns throwing open their doors and the wine and ale flowed freely through the streets as people celebrated. Not everyone cheered this turn of events, however, and some quietly went back to their homes without comment. But as the celebrations began to die down a solemn and heavy weight began to descend on us all. It was now official, we are at war with England, the most powerful nation in the world.

Chapter Eleven

Les Beaux Français

It has been nearly a year since we declared independence from Britain and the war is centered now in the New York and New Jersey colonies. Sadly, New York has fallen to the British and the Hessians, German soldiers, have joined in the fight. Some have been able to flee New York and we have taken in as many women and children in Boston as we can. For several weeks now there has been fierce fighting at Fort Stanwix in New York but the Continentals have successfully held off the British charge and that has buoyed morale.

There is a new presence in the city in the last few weeks, a contingent of Frenchmen can be seen on the streets in the company of the Patriot leaders and it should have been of no surprise to me when

Benjamin asked if one of the men could join us for dinner, to which I happily agreed.

When Benjamin arrived with his companion, I must say I was taken aback, the man with him was certainly one of the most handsome men I had ever seen. His hair was very dark, nearly black with wavy curls that were held together in a beautiful ribbon. His complexion was smooth and unlined, and he had very long lashes on his light brown eyes which seemed to glow of an inner light. He was of medium height and slim build and his clothes were made of finest brocade. His shirt was a fine white linen with a cascade of ruffles ending in wide cuffs held together with beautiful silver pins. I felt rather plain and unadorned next to this man despite the fact that I was wearing the best dress that I owned.

"Mother, may I present Monsieur Jean-Baptiste dit Beauchamp. He is the special envoy of Charles Gravier, Comte de Vergennes, the French Foreign Minister."

"Monsieur Beauchamp, it is my pleasure to meet you and an honor to have you dine with us in our home," I said, extending my hand.

He bowed with a flourish over my hand before he spoke in nearly perfect English but with a heavy French accent.

"Madam Parkman, I am the one who is most honored to be in the company of such a fine patriot as your son Benjamin, and the beautiful woman who raised such a fine gentleman," he replied, kissing my hand gently, which I am not ashamed to admit made my heart skip a beat.

"Jean, my sister, Miss Amelia Parkman," said Benjamin as Amelia stepped forward into the light. She shone like a diamond, and although no longer a young girl, she was more beautiful than ever, even without the jewels that had once adorned her neck, which were sold to pay for Simon's journey back to England.

Monsieur Beauchamp stepped forward to take Amelia's hand, but he said nothing as he looked into her eyes. She held his gaze, and I could see her own eyes softening as she looked into his.

"Mademoiselle Parkman, I never imagined when your brother regaled me with tales of your daring efforts during the siege that he would neglect to share with me that you are not only brave, but you are also most beautiful," he said as he brought her hand up to his lips, kissing it gently while still gazing into her eyes.

"Vous me flattez Monsieur Beauchamp, et je vous remercie très sincèrement de vos attentions," responded Amelia in her perfect French accent.

"Your French is beautiful Mademoiselle. Benjamin, you did not tell me your sister spoke French!" chided the Monsieur, still holding onto Amelia's hand.

"I had forgotten that she did!" said Benjamin laughing.

"Please let us sit for dinner," I said as I motioned toward the dining room.

Monsieur Beauchamp expertly took Amelia's arm and guided her to the dining room. After seating her, he immediately occupied the chair directly across from her. I could not help but smile, it reminded me of John and Antoinette the first time they met in this house and just like with the two of them, I could see these two were clearly smitten with each other.

"Monsieur Beauchamp, what brings you to Boston?" I asked as Fiona poured some wine.

"Jean please, Madam Parkman, you must call me Jean," he said with a nod in my direction.

"Of course, if you wish."

Jean raised his wine glass, "A toast to Madam Parkman our gracious host, to my new friend Benjamin, and to the beautiful Mademoiselle Parkman."

"Amelia, please call me Amelia."

"Amelia, it is a fair and lovely name is it not?"

"Merci Jean, merci," replied Amelia, now blushing nearly crimson.

"Now to your question, Madame, I am here on behalf of the French government to talk with the Continental Army to see how the French might be of assistance in this conflict against the tyrants in London."

"Since the British have formed an alliance with the Hessians against us, we thought we might also avail ourselves of an alliance to strengthen our forces and France has approached us. Obviously, there is no affection between England and France, and we could most certainly use their help," added Benjamin.

I could understand why the French disliked the English so much, they have a long history of conflicts between them, most recently the war here in the colonies which took the life of Simon William and drove the French out of the Ohio Valley. I wonder if Jean was at all uncomfortable with the knowledge that a member of our family had fought against the French not that many years ago, or perhaps he did not know.

"We are not enamored with the English as you say Benjamin, and we welcome the opportunity to support you in your cause for liberty."

"Did you know, Jean, that our older brother, Simon William, fought for the British in the French and Indian War?" asked Amelia hesitatingly.

"I am aware, Mademoiselle Amelia, and to you and your family I give my condolences, for Benjamin has told me of your loss. Please know that I do not blame the colonies, nor this family, for the war brought against us by the British. Your brother was acting with honor and courage, and that can never be something to disdain," said Jean, bowing his head to each of us in turn.

"Thank you, Jean, that is most kind of you," I said, relieved that this would not be a secret between us.

"The French are here now to observe but our hope is that they will support us with arms and men eventually," said Benjamin.

"When will you be leaving?" asked Amelia.

"Soon, we need another fortnight to finish preparing everything for the journey south," replied Jean.

"So, you will stay until all is ready?" she asked not so coyly.

"I will," he said as he smiled at her causing her to blush once again.

"Benjamin, are you going to New Jersey as well?" I asked, perhaps already knowing in my heart what he would say.

"I am mother, but do not worry. Hamish will continue to keep an eye on you and ensure you are safe, although this time it will not be in secret," he said smiling.

The conversation turned to more pleasant things and Jean told us all about his home outside Paris and his family. He and Amelia exchanged occasional phrases in French and there was much laughter and plenty of wine. I had not felt this happy in some time, and it was wonderful to see Amelia and Benjamin so happy as well. As Jean prepared to leave, he hesitated by the front door.

"Mademoiselle Amelia, with your permission and of course that of your mother and brother, may I call on you again, perhaps tomorrow?"

"Bien sûr, tu peux, je l'attends avec impatience, of course you may, I look forward to it," she added in English for my benefit.

He bowed and kissed her hand once again before bidding us all a good night. Amelia practically danced her way up the stairs and Benjamin and I could hardly contain our laughter. Amelia is not one to be easily impressed by men and so this was quite a turn of events, but one I was happy to see. I could not help, however, to ruminate on the fact that both he and Benjamin would be leaving soon to join the fighting and I did not want for her the heartbreak that follows war like a shadow following the setting sun. Many men have already fought and died in this conflict and there will be many more before it is over. I could only hope that God would not come for any more of my sons.

Jean came every day without fail and he and Amelia talked endlessly while I sat with the other women sewing in the parlor. All the women gossiped endlessly about how handsome all of the Frenchmen are who were in town, but especially about Jean-Baptiste Beauchamp whose name seemed to be on everyone's lips. Perhaps it was just that our men no longer dressed in their finest clothes and were often unshaven, that we are so easily attracted to a well-dressed, impeccably groomed, and handsome man. It was a pleasant distraction to be sure but yesterday I heard that preparations are complete, and I know that means that Jean and Benjamin will be leaving tomorrow, and my heart is filled with dread once again. Before they go, however, we will have one last dinner together with the four of us. I was still getting ready when Benjamin knocked at my door.

"Mother, may I come in?"

"Yes dear, I am almost ready, but come," I replied as I sat in front of the mirror finishing my hair.

He closed the door behind him.

"Mother, Jean has asked to speak to you privately before dinner," he said with a sly grin on his face.

"Benjamin, you do not mean he intends to ask for Amelia's hand, do you?" I said with surprise.

"I believe he does mother; he has already spoken to me on the matter. I have inquired of others as to his family and his means and I am satisfied. I have given him my blessing but told him he must speak to you."

"But son, they have only known each other a short time. I know they are both quite taken with each other, but still."

"How long did you know father before you married him?" he asked.

"All right Benjamin, your argument is well taken, but your father was not leaving to go to war, and we spent several more months courting before the wedding."

"They do not have to marry the moment he returns, mother, assuming of course he does return," he said thoughtfully.

"Oh, Benjamin, why would you say such a thing?" I asked distressed.

"I am sorry mother, but we both know it is a possibility that neither of us will return. I did not mean to cause you sorrow," he said as he kissed me on top of the head.

I reached up and clasped his hand, now resting on my shoulder. It was rough and calloused, and gunpowder always seemed to linger beneath his fingernails no matter how much he washed his hands. It was a strong hand, a capable hand.

"You must come home to me, my son; I do not think I could bear it if you do not."

"I promise, mother, to do my very best to do so but it is in the hands of General Washington and God, and I have faith in them both."

"Do you believe that Amelia wishes for me to approve of this betrothal?" I asked at last.

"I believe she does, mother."

"I wish your father were here, he would know what to do," I said sadly. In this moment, I missed Simon more than I did even in the quiet of the night. His daughter was the most precious thing on earth to him, he would know if this was right. Benjamin kissed me on the cheek.

"You always do the right thing mother, and father trusted you implicitly, you will know what to do if you listen to your heart. Father's voice will be there for you to hear," he said as he turned and left the room.

I looked at my reflection in the mirror. Simon did trust me, but I am not sure I always deserved that trust, having kept from him some things he should have known, but I did so for the sake of my family. My face was showing its age as I was not far now from my sixtieth year on this earth, and the lines have taken hold. I could not help but think about how much I looked like my mother, and the thought of it made me smile. I had always looked so much like my mother, and many said she looked very much like her mother. It was a badge I was proud to wear. Fiona knocked at the door.

"Ma'am, Monsieur Beauchamp is here," she said. "Do you need any help?"

"No Fiona, thank you I am done. Please show him to the study," I said as I stood and smoothed my dress. The same dress I had worn that night for dinner so many years ago when Josiah Hutton had joined us with his Aunt Mary and Antoinette. It was Simon's favorite, and the memory brought me comfort, and hopefully strength to make the right decision.

Jean was waiting by Simon's desk looking at a map on the wall when I entered, and he turned and bowed to me gracefully.

"Madam Parkman you are especially lovely this evening, your gown matches the beautiful blue of your eyes," he said as he kissed my hand.

His comment took my breath away, it was the same exact thing Simon had said to me the first time I wore this dress.

"Thank you, Jean, this dress was my husband's favorite," I said, pleased by his observation.

"It is obvious why," he said as he led me to the couch and helped me to be seated before sitting next to me and taking one of my hands in both of his.

"Madame, I wanted to speak to you on a most serious matter, a matter of the heart," he said sincerely.

I nodded.

"A child is the most precious thing which a mother or father has, they are angels sent from heaven to bless us and to make our lives full beyond measure. Your angel, Mademoiselle Amelia, has touched my heart beyond measure, and I have grown to love her deeply these last few weeks. I know it is much to ask of a mother to give one of her angels, and you do not know me well. I am a man of good character from a family of fine standing and of means. We are honest hard-working people. More importantly, we are a family who have deep respect and love for each other as I do for Amelia. Tomorrow, we will depart to join the fray but before I go, I must ask your permission to propose to Amelia. I do not know how much life God is willing to grant me, but I do know that whatever that is, may it be short or long, I do not want to live it without her by my side."

As I looked into his eyes, I could see he was most sincere, and I took a deep breath as I quietly listened to my heart.

"You have my blessing," I said softly.

"Ma très chère Madame, je vous suis à jamais redevable, j'aimerai et chérirai votre fille jusqu'à mon dernier jour," he exclaimed.

"In English please, Jean," I said smiling.

"Oh yes, my apologies. When I am excited, I speak only French!

My dearest Madam, I am forever in your debt. I will love and cherish your daughter to my very last breath," he said as he kissed me on each cheek.

"I will send Amelia to you," I said as I rose to my feet and Jean could not help but kiss me again and it was all I could do not to break into peals of laughter.

Benjamin and I waited at a discreet distance as Jean spoke to Amelia in the library, in French so we knew very little of what was being said but it was obvious that Amelia was delighted.

"Benjamin, did you not take French in school also?" I asked with a whisper.

"I did mother, but I do not recall a word!" he replied with a wink.

It was a wonderful evening of celebration and Amelia was so pleased to show her posey ring to everyone, inscribed in French of course, with the words "pour l'amour et la fidélité" which means for love and fidelity. How Jean was able to get that done here in Boston was beyond comprehension, but it seems that Paul Revere, the renowned Patriot and silversmith here in Boston, came to his aid at Benjamin's request. It was a bittersweet night too and it was clear that Jean was reluctant to leave. It was nearly dawn when he and Benjamin finally headed to the meeting point to begin their trek south.

Amelia cried quietly on and off all day, but I could not find words to comfort her. We were both feeling the pain of their departure and all we could do now was pray for their safe return. Jean had promised to write as often as he could, and I know that will be some comfort to Amelia. We dare not speak of plans for the wedding so as to not hex the future and so we focused instead on continuing our work to support the troops.

One just need walk around town or to the market to notice there are far fewer men in town than just a few days before. The very young, the men too old or feeble to fight, or those who still quietly try to maintain their loyalty to England remained. It now fell heavily to the women of Boston to run the local council and to ensure the town's readiness.

We worked with Hamish, who had stayed behind to keep the tavern open, as he showed us the proper way to use a musket, to load our powder and musket balls, even how to make musket balls if need be. While we were all becoming much better at using the musket only a few women had even attempted to take on the task of making musket balls. I found the whole process to be terrifying and I was grateful that others had chosen that task.

I received a letter today from Antoinette to tell me that John had been killed fighting in New York. The paper felt as though it weighed several stone, the same as the weight now on my heart. God has taken another son fighting in defense of the Crown, and for what, because King George could not see his way clear to treat us as equal to other Englishmen. I retreated to my room with the letter in hand, I could not bear the thought of telling my children that they had lost another brother. Quietly, I sat looking at the letter over and over again as if somehow the words on the page would change. I am grateful that Simon is not here to learn that he has lost another son, it would break his heart too.

"Mrs. Parkman, it is time for dinner," said Fiona as she cracked open the door.

"Not tonight, Fiona, please join Amelia so she does not eat alone."

"Yes ma'am," she replied as she quietly shut the door.

I was still sitting in the same spot when Amelia came to my door.

"Mother?"

"Yes, my dear, come in."

"Mother why are you sitting in the dark?" she asked as she lit the lamp.

"Antoinette has written to me. Your brother…" I said as I handed her the letter. I could not even speak the words.

She read it slowly and as I did, she read it again hoping the message would be a different one. She leaned back in her chair and sighed loudly but, surprisingly, she did not cry.

"I loved John despite the fact that I did not agree with what I saw as his displaced loyalty and I know that in part his desire was to honor father, as you did. But in the end, we all live, and die, by the faith of our convictions and the truth we must find for ourselves. John was happy to give his life in defense of the Crown just as Benjamin, Nathaniel and I would be happy to give our lives in the battle for liberty and equality.

While I do not agree with his choice, I respect … respected it. I never felt less love for him because of it, but I am not sure that is truly what he would say about me. My belief is that he did not understand my choices and did not respect them or me. It is a sadness to me that we parted with our last words being angry ones. I am sorry, mother, that once again you have lost a son to war, and I pray most fervently that God will not ask it of you again."

With that, she kissed me on the cheek and quietly left the room. My tears came for the first time, but I felt no relief from the deluge. It saddens me more than I can say that John felt his family had turned on him, especially Amelia. I had hoped that at some point we could all be together and find a way to heal this rift, but sadly it now will never be. Antoinette has said she will stay in Nova Scotia where she has the support of the other wives and officers, and I am glad that she has found a place that she can call her home. I know now that I will never see John's children again and I can only pray for their welfare and happiness.

The next week's post brought much happier news. Nathaniel has married the niece of John Adams, a young woman named Emily, and she is with child. They were forced to flee Philadelphia when the British captured the city, and they are now in hiding with others of the Continental Congress, meeting in secret to organize the government. It is a comfort to know he is safe, and not alone, and that his efforts now are behind the lines of fighting rather than on them.

Benjamin remains with Washington as does Jean-Baptiste and they both write when they can. Conditions have been difficult, disease swept through the camp during the cold winter months and many, many soldiers died of sickness. There have been some losses and some gains as the war teeters between the two armies, but we are still far from an end to the conflict. Supplies continue to arrive in Boston regularly to be carted off to the encampments and I try with each shipment to include a letter, one from me and one from Amelia for Jean. I do not know if anyone expected that the war would be over quickly, but I think few were prepared to see the second anniversary of the Battle of Lexington and Concord come and go some months past.

Amelia is stalwart and steadfast, but she longs now for a child, and it is my hope that Jean may return soon so that they can marry. For myself, I wish for nothing, only that my children and grandchildren are safe and well. That is all I need; that is all I will ever need.

Chapter Twelve

Subterfuge

The days are starting to grow shorter, and the air has taken on the cool crispness that comes with fall. The leaves on the trees are starting to change, transforming from green to every shade of red, orange, and brown. Amelia and I have been apple picking and, in a few days, we will begin canning to fill our larder for the winter. Hamish brought us half a hog a few weeks ago and that will do nicely for the next few months. I was most concerned when I saw him, he looked thin, and he coughed without relief for most of the time we were together. His days may be numbered I fear, as I suppose they are for us all. You never know how many days are ahead, but I know there are more now behind me than in front of me.

The women have not met to sew for a few weeks, but a request has come for two dozen more uniforms and so the parlor is full once again as we chatter and stitch. We have become a family of sorts these many months, sisters really, and it is a blessing to have their support and comfort. I could never have imagined how a knock on the door this morning would change it all.

"Mrs. Parkman, there is a young man here. He is looking for Benjamin," said Fiona.

"Show him in Fiona, he can come here, I have no secrets from these women," I said.

The young man, a boy really, looked to be about the age of thirteen or so, rather dirty and unkempt but well spoken.

"Mrs. Parkman, I have a message for Master Benjamin," said the boy in a voice bigger than I was expecting.

"You are?

"I am Amos Foster, ma'am."

"And Amos, your message is from whom?"

"From my father, we live outside of town along the coast, and he is a watchman for the Continentals.

He keeps an eye and ear out for British ships that might try to land outside the harbor."

"I see, what is it that your father wishes for Benjamin to know?"

"There is a British ship anchored offshore and talk is that a small number of soldiers intend to come ashore with evil intent."

"And what would that intent be?" asked Mrs. Keene.

"To burn the Boston wharf so that no ships will be able to land there with supplies for the army," he said.

We all looked at each other in horror. If ships could not get into Boston harbor it would severely hamper our armies' efforts, it might even cost us the war.

"How is it they intend to accomplish that?" asked Amelia.

"We do not know for certain but a Mr. White, a man still loyal to the crown, has recently purchased several new horses. My father thinks they will come ashore and then ride to Boston."

"How many horses does Mr. White have?" I asked.

"Ten, Mrs. Parkman, he has ten but only a few weeks ago he had only six."

"So why are you here to tell Benjamin, will you not organize to confront them when they come ashore?"

"No ma'am, there is just my father who is loyal to the cause and a few much older men who are not able to fight. Everyone else in our small town is loyal to the crown. My father was always told to let Benjamin know if there was trouble."

"I understand, thank you, Amos. Fiona, would you get this young man some food and drink please."

"Amelia, we need to talk to Hamish at once. Ladies, you are welcome to stay, we will be back as soon as we can."

We walked quickly through town and arrived at the tavern in just a few minutes. Mrs. Ayers was busy serving the few men seated at small round tables, so we went to the back on our own to find Hamish lying in the same bed I had once lain in. He was pale and his breathing was labored, the spittoon on the side of the bed was filled with spit and blood.

"Hamish, we need to talk to you," I said, as I pulled up a chair next to him. He nodded and I quickly explained what young Amos had told me. He moaned as he rubbed his eyes with his hands.

"This is no good, no good t'all," he said finally.

"Why Hamish, what do you mean," I said, my voice rising with concern, not just for him but for all of us.

"There is a small group of men, these be men we trust, trained in such things, ya know," he said with labored breath.

Amelia let out a huge sigh of relief.

"Do not be relieved yet, missy, yer help is not here. They have gone north, where there is also a ship offshore, to be sure no mischief happens."

"Surely, Hamish, there must be others who can help?"

"No, none that we can say we trust with certainty," he said, moaning as he rubbed his face again.

Amelia and I looked at each other and I could see the panic and fear in her eyes. There must be something we can do; we cannot just sit by and do nothing. We may have to take a chance on men whose loyalties are uncertain and hope for the best.

"Hamish, how would these men get into town from Belmont, the place Amos Foster is from?" asked Amelia thoughtfully.

"There tis only one way Miss Amelia, the marshes take all but one road and there is a bridge they must cross, but if they make it to this side, there will be no stopin' them."

"Thank you, Hamish, you rest now," said Amelia as she motioned toward the door.

"Come mother, I have an idea," she said.

Amelia insisted we wait until we got home to tell me about her plan as she says it involves all the sewing circle women. Once at home, we filled everyone in on what Hamish had said and Amelia, at last, was ready to share her plan.

"I was thinking that if men could pretend to be Indians, then why could women not pretend to be men?" she said at last.

We looked at each other in disbelief, trying to comprehend what she was suggesting.

"Amelia, surely you do not expect us to go and fight these trained soldiers?" asked Mary.

"But what if we did?" asked Cynthia cautiously.

"What if we did not fight them at all but rather, we simply blocked their path?" asked Mrs. Keene. Mrs. Brown nodded in agreement.

"What if we used a wagon or two and some hay to block the bridge?' I proposed.

"They would just push it out of the way," said Mary.

"Not if they thought soldiers with muskets were on the other side," said Fiona as she gestured to the pile of uniforms.

"Surely you are not suggesting we disguise ourselves as soldiers and fight them?" asked Martha, aghast at the suggestion.

"We could simply stuff the uniforms with hay to make them look like people and set muskets up on the bales," suggested Cynthia.

"No, I think if we are to be successful, there must be real people in those uniforms," I said at last. "If we place the wagons just inside the bridge and use bales to build a wall, we can crouch behind it to fire on them when they get close."

"And when they fire back?" asked Martha.

"The bales should give us the protection that we need," said Amelia.

"I believe mother is right, this is the only way. The men have done all they can, now it is up to us."

We all sat for a few minutes, each deep in their own thoughts. Could we really do this, could I? Are we prepared to take the lives of these men should they try to cross the bridge into Boston?

"Ladies, we have come to trust and rely on one another these many, many months. Now I believe we must rely on each other again as the very fate of our nation, this war, may hang in the balance. If the harbor is destroyed, it will have a devastating effect, of that I have no doubt. We do not have time to send word to try and get aid, we must act, we must act together, and we must act now. If anyone here does not wish to participate, you may leave now and there will be no animosity toward you," I said, looking at Martha.

"I cannot Eliza, I wish that I could, but my Quaker beliefs will not allow me to take the life of another. I will pray for you all," said Martha as she gathered her things and left.

We spent the rest of the day getting ready, as we did not know for sure when the soldiers would attempt to cross, but we knew we had to be there before nightfall if it was today. With some difficulty, we were able to load two wagons with hay, it would be much easier getting them out. There would be just the seven of us, Mary, Fiona, Mrs. Brown, Mrs. Keene, Cynthia, Amelia, and I, it would have to be enough. We decided to stuff a few extra uniforms to make our numbers look larger and we threw the extra "men" into the back of the wagon with the hay.

Between us we had eleven muskets and adequate shot and powder. If there was fighting, it would not last long and so we had what we needed. As the sun was low in the western sky, we set off in two wagons bound for Belmont. Amos went along with us and helped us blockade the bridge with the wagons and build a wall of hay. Then he took the horses so they would not be in harm's way and went ahead to his farm to let his father know what we were doing. They would do their best to try and alert us if they saw any soldiers headed toward the bridge. Once they entered the bridge, Mr. Foster and Amos would move onto the road to prevent any attempt to bypass the bridge.

It was a long chilly night as we took turns keeping watch, and our only company was the calls of those animals who come to life after dark. There was no talking, no sound, and we dared not build a fire as we did not want to risk being seen by them before they entered the bridge. There was little moon this night, the sky full of clouds that blocked any light there might have been. I ached from sitting on the cold hard ground all night leaning against a hay bale. We took turns keeping watch but truly no one slept. We were each captive to our own thoughts and fears, and we talked only in very quiet whispers and hushed voices. This had happened so quickly we did not really have time to be afraid, but I have no doubt fear resides in the heart of every woman this night.

The sun rose bright in the sky after a long quiet night, and knowing they would not risk trying to cross in the daylight we could rest a bit and make a small fire to warm some stew. We could only hope no one else would try to cross from either side, forcing us to move our barricade, or worse yet, a loyalist who might alert the British when they came ashore. If they were to learn we were here, they could go around by land to reach Boston. It would take much longer and be more dangerous, but if they did there would be no way we could protect ourselves from an attack. There would be too much ground to cover.

We spent the day checking and double-checking our muskets and trying to steel our nerves for another night to come. Mrs. Keene had brought a small flask of brandy and, as night fell, we passed it from woman to woman, each of us taking a sip. The brandy warmed me and helped to steady my nerves. I was grateful that, as night fell, I found myself standing watch next to Amelia.

"Are you frightened, mother?" she said in a voice so low it was barely a whisper.

"Only for you, my dear," I said in an equally quiet whisper as I squeezed her arm.

"You are not afraid of dying?"

"No, I am only afraid of failing. We have come so far in this fight, and we are getting closer and closer to realizing the dream of controlling our own destiny. I will never hesitate again to defend this land with my very life if that is what it will take."

"Father would be very proud of you," she said.

"Do you think so?"

"I do mother, right before he left, as I was helping him write the letters for Nathaniel and Benjamin, he told me he knew what I had done. He also told me he was proud of me and of you, for listening to our hearts and doing what we believed was right."

"He was not angry that I had kept that from him?" I asked, afraid almost to hear the reply.

"No mother, he understood you were trying to protect him, protect the family, and he loved you for it."

"Thank you, Amelia, that warms my heart so very much."

"Mother?"

"Yes dear?"

"Look," she said, pointing off to the right of the bridge.

"That is the signal from Amos," I said, "they are coming."

"So they are, I love you mother, with all my heart. I will wake the others," said Amelia as I picked up my musket and took my position.

They were quickly on their feet and we each took the spot we had chosen for ourselves. The creatures of the night chirped all around us, but in a few minutes we also heard something else, the faint sounds of men on horseback. There was almost no moon which worked to our advantage in that they would not be able to see the barricade till they were on the bridge. Each woman took up her position along the hay wall as we focused our attention on the bridge ahead.

"I realize, Mrs. Keene and Mrs. Brown, I do not know your given names," I said, without taking my eyes off the road.

"Elizabeth," whispered Mrs. Keene to my right.

"Meredith," whispered Mrs. Brown to my left.

"It is my honor to serve our country with all of you," I said, as I began to hear the clomping of hooves on the wooden bridge.

"Remember, do not fire until I say so," I said, trying to calm my breathing. There were four muskets in reserve, loaded and ready to go. Our best shots, Cynthia, Mary, Fiona, and Amelia would take those after discharging their first weapon. Elizabeth, Meredith, and I would have to reload. I could hear men's voices now but could not tell what they were saying. I peeked up over the bale and I could see they were still less than halfway across; we needed them to come closer as our aim was certainly not the best.

The sound of men laughing filtered across the night air and I knew that meant they had not seen the barricade yet, or perhaps they were laughing at its rudimentary construction, but either way it meant they were getting closer. I was sure I could hear my own heart beating as we stood perfectly still, waiting. If we fire too soon, we may miss them, if we wait too long, they will be on top of us, and all may be lost. *God be with us and protect us…*

"Now!" I shouted.

In unison we all rose, raised our muskets, and fired. The noise was deafening, and the acrid smoke filled my nostrils. My ears were ringing but I could still hear the sounds of horses and men reacting to the barrage. They immediately returned our fire, musket balls colliding with the bales and wagon as splintered wood flew over our heads. I could hear screaming and shouting and then I heard gunfire from the other side of the bridge. Mr. Foster and Amos were firing as well.

"Again!" I screamed over the din as the second rounds were fired from our side.

Cynthia screamed as she fell to the ground, her clothes instantly stained with blood. But Elizabeth did not stop to tend to her, she had reloaded, and she fired again as did Meredith and me. A musket ball hit directly in front of me, and a large splinter of wood pierced my left arm just above the elbow. No matter, I kept reloading and we each fired two more volleys. I was about to reload again when Amelia grabbed my arm and, suddenly, I realized no one was shooting back, it was quiet.

"Stop!" I said as I held up my hand and listened. I heard one shot being fired on the bridge, but it did not seem to be aimed at us. We waited, hardly breathing.

"Mrs. Parkman," came a man's voice, "Do not shoot, it is Mr. Foster and Amos. It is done, they are all dead."

I dropped my musket and turned my attention to Cynthia who lay crying on the ground near me. Amelia lit the lantern as Cynthia's mother and I tore open her clothes to find the source of the bleeding which we were able to staunch with some bandages we had brought.

"Mother, you are bleeding," said Amelia as she held the lantern up to me. Her face was splattered with blood, I am not sure whose.

"It is nothing," I said as Amelia tried to bandage around the large wooden splinter protruding from my arm. The blood had seeped down my entire sleeve and was dripping off the ends of my fingers.

Mr. Foster and Amos had broken through the barricade, and he was helping tend to Cynthia as Amelia and I stepped around the bales to survey the bridge. There were dead horses and dead men lying everywhere and more blood than I had ever seen, even when we had gone to Nathaniel's aid. There was so much blood in such a small space that it formed small rivers and oozed off the sides of the bridge and into the murky marsh below. A couple of the horses had retreated to the far end of the bridge and stood there, riderless, waiting for direction. I counted nine men in all, no ten, and some who looked no older than Amos and one who looked unnervingly like John.

The moon had just peeked out now, as if it too, had been hiding waiting to make an appearance. The light only made the ghastly scene more surreal.

"Amelia, look away, go back and help the others," I said, not wanting her to see any more of this than necessary.

I could hear one of the other women crying quietly as another tried to comfort her. I could not help but mourn for these men, for they are each a father, brother, husband, or son. Their families would not know where they would lie in our soil, only that they had died fighting a war between those who shared the same bonds of ancestry, the same history, the same blood.

The sight of the carnage combined with my own loss of blood caused my stomach to churn and I retched there on the side of the bridge. *Why, why did it have to come to this,* I was screaming in my head before a sound like the waves of the ocean filled my ears and I stumbled forward, falling on the ground before the darkness enfolded me.

Chapter Thirteen

Scattered to the Wind

The sun shone brightly through my bedroom windows as Fiona pulled back the curtains. I did not know how, but I was here in my own bed, my left arm throbbing with pain and heavily bandaged.

"You are awake ma'am," said Fiona smiling.

"Fiona, I think it is time you called me Eliza," I said as I tried to sit up.

"Oh no ma'am, I do not think I could do that," she said with a giggle more suited to a schoolgirl than a woman more than half my age.

"Fiona, considering what we have been through together I feel it is only right, so try, please?"

"Of course, Mrs. Eliza," she said smiling.

Well, it was a start at least. I lay back against the pillow realizing that to rise from this bed would require more strength than I had at this moment. Fiona told me that Cynthia was also recovering at home, and that Elizabeth came to see me today and assured her that she will survive this ordeal, for which I am most grateful. I will try to call on her as soon as I can. Some of the other women had minor injuries but nothing of concern. An elderly man from the Boston Gazette had come to talk to Amelia a few days ago and apparently now our escapades are the talk of the town and praise was flowing at us from every direction. I wish that had not happened. I felt no pleasure in taking the lives of others, enemy or not, and I did not feel we deserved to be treated as heroes when men were doing heroic things every day without attention.

I have been resting a great deal and it has been nearly two weeks since our attack at the bridge and I am able to spend more of my day out of bed than in it. My arm is still quite painful. The Doctor says it will continue to improve but will likely never be the same. It is no matter; it is a very small price to pay for protecting the harbor.

"Mrs. Eliza, you have a visitor," said Fiona with a grin she could not hide. Behind her in the doorway was a figure I recognized immediately, and I jumped to my feet.

"Benjamin!"

"Good day. mother," he said as he embraced me.

"Ow," I winced as he squeezed my left arm too tightly.

"Mother, I did not know you had been hurt?" he said with concern.

"It is nothing, son. Truly, I am so happy to see you but what are you doing here?"

"The army is wintering in now and Jean and I thought we would spend the winter here with you instead of with that lot of smelly, dirty men," he said smiling. "Also, we heard about what you and the other women did to save the port, and General Washington wanted us to bring you his sincere thanks, because if we had lost the harbor, we would lose this war."

"Benjamin, I am humbled by his thanks, but it is no more than any of you would have done, and we are all just relieved that we were successful, and we all survived. "Jean is here too?"

"He is, he and Amelia are in the kitchen, I wanted to surprise you."

"Well, you have done that my dearest and it is a wonderful, wonderful surprise indeed."

Amelia and Jean joined us in the parlor, and it was a joyous reunion and warmed my heart. As I had anticipated, Amelia and Jean wanted to marry as quickly as possible and this time there was no hesitation on my part. We would make arrangements within the next couple of days, and we could move them into the room previously occupied by John and Antoinette. Dinner that evening was a joyous affair and Benjamin even had a letter from Nathaniel telling us of the birth of his son who he named Josiah Simon Parkman. His father would have been very proud of him, indeed of all his children and hopefully of me.

Amelia, Fiona, and I spent all the next day trying to decide on something for Amelia to wear while Benjamin and Jean made arrangements at the church.

"Mother, none of these things are right, I just do not know what I am going to do," whined Amelia, rather uncharacteristically for her.

Women start thinking about the day they will marry when they are little girls and often those dreams are hard to reconcile with the reality of the day when it comes.

"Mrs. Eliza, I have a suggestion?" said Fiona thoughtfully.

"Yes Fiona?"

"The dress you wore when you married Master Simon is packed away in a trunk in the attic…"

"My goodness Fiona you are right, I had forgotten that."

"Can we get it down?" asked Amelia.

I nodded and the three of us practically ran up to the attic to find the dress. Fiona dragged a trunk out of the far corner of the attic where it had sat undisturbed all these years. I wiped away the dust and slowly opened the lid. Inside, wrapped carefully in muslin, was a pale pink confection trimmed with lace and pearls.

"Oh mother, it is beautiful," gushed Amelia as she held the dress up and admired it.

"It may be a bit too short for you, but we could add another row of lace on the bottom, there is a bit of extra here in the trunk.

"It is perfect mother; may I wear it? Please?"

"Of course darling, I would be delighted," I said smiling.

The day of the wedding was cold but clear and it did nothing to dampen our spirits. My only regret this day is that Simon and all of Amelia's brothers were not here for her. Fiona and Benjamin stood with the couple and there were just a few of us in the pews but it was perfect in every way. Amelia was stunning and Jean-Baptiste was even more handsome if one could believe that was possible. He shed a few tears when he first saw his bride and I must say I did the same. Only Benjamin now remains unmarried, and I am hoping he will resume his interest in Amelia's former student, Miss Stevens, as she is still unmarried.

Richard has not remarried but he has kept in contact with me these last few years and he seems to live a happy life in Barbados. He says he will come to visit us when the war is over, but we will see. I am simply glad he is well and happy. He managed to find other buyers for the molasses produced at the estate and so in that way he has kept Simon's legacy and business alive, and I am very proud of him for his efforts.

Nathaniel intends to take a role in the new government continuing to work for John Adams, but I do not know where that means he will reside. This house is starting to feel rather large, and I know that Jean has always been clear that he intends to return to France at some point in the not-too-distant future. He has family obligations there, an estate that also needs his attention. As much as Amelia loves Boston, I know she is very excited about the prospect. Perhaps it is time for me to think about what I would like to do with what is left of my life. It seems the house will go to Benjamin, and I know that it will be safe in his care. He intends to have a blacksmithing business here when the war is over, and Boston will be his home for the foreseeable future.

The winter passes quietly, with many nights playing cards and laughing around the table. The more I have gotten to know Jean, the more I know that

Amelia has made the right choice. He is a thoughtful husband and surely he will make a good father, in about seven months' time as it happens. Benjamin says it will be only one or two more weeks before he will rejoin General Washington, but I was not prepared for the conversation at dinner that night.

"Benjamin, your sister and I have had much discussion these last few weeks, and we have decided it is best if I leave you now and return to France. I will not be going south with you again, my friend."

"Jean, I thought you would wait until later in the year!" said Benjamin, clearly surprised.

"It is true that was my desire, until God decided to bestow upon us this new life. I would like my child to be born in France, you understand this, yes?" asked Jean.

"Of course, I understand, you have been of tremendous help to us and I for one will sorely miss your company. But I respect your decision, I am sure I would feel the same way as you do."

"Mother, we wanted to talk to you also," said Amelia hesitantly. "We are hoping you will consider coming with us to France."

"That is very kind of you Amelia, Jean, and I would be lying if I said I had not already considered it. But I cannot leave this house until Benjamin returns and I know that it is in good hands."

"Could you not leave Fiona to manage the house until Benjamin can return?" asked Jean.

"I am sure, mother, that Fiona could make do, there is little that she cannot manage. I know that Mr. Brown would be willing to assist with the barn and things that may need repair as he and I have spoken of it," added Benjamin.

"I will think on it," I said. "For now let us not talk about parting but instead enjoying the time we have left together. Jean, when will you and Amelia be leaving?"

"The first ships will begin to sail again in early March just a few weeks or so after Benjamin must leave."

"Well, I will give you my decision within the week so that we all will know what is to be done before anyone departs."

That night, as I sat in front of the mirror brushing out my hair, my reflection reminded me again that my time was growing short. Staying with Amelia and seeing her through this transition to her new life is important to be sure, I do not want her to feel alone in a strange place. But now, after we have gone through so much to fight for this land, this place I love so much, can I really leave it?

Today we learned that the French, who have been covertly supplying the Continentals with arms, men, and expertise for the last couple of years, have officially declared their alliance with us in our fight against the British. This means that as Jean and Amelia head east, more and more of his country-men from the French army will be headed west. It was great news and Benjamin is most relieved as he prepares to leave for Valley Forge in a couple of days.

"Mother, I wanted to tell you that I intend to propose to Hannah Stevens tomorrow before I go," he said as we sat quietly together in the study.

"That is wonderful news Benjamin, I am very happy for you, the Stevens are a wonderful family, and your father was very close to her father."

"Thank you, mother, it is a good match I believe, and it heartens me to know that father would approve."

"He most certainly would, my son."

"I always feel closer to him when I sit in this room," said Benjamin as he looked around at all the mementos of Simon's life, left very much as they were the day he departed.

"I do too, I often come in the evening and sit here alone. I miss him still very much."

"Have you decided if you will go with Amelia and Jean," asked Benjamin.

"I have determined that I will not go. Boston is my home, and I cannot leave it. It is my most fervent belief that you and the Continental Army will prevail, and I want to be here, if God grants me his grace, to enjoy the fruits of that labor. When you return, I will move to the smaller house which we had bought for John and Antoinette. It still sits empty, and it will be just enough for me. You and Hannah can have this place, it is time for its next Parkman family."

"Mother, you know you do not need to do that, you will be more than welcome to stay here with us," said Benjamin as he took my hand in his.

"I know my son, but Hannah needs to be the mistress of her own home. She does not need me looking over her shoulder," I said smiling.

"I am sure, mother, that she would not feel that way about it, but you do what pleases you."

"I must tell you though, my son, that I am keeping Fiona with me," I said with all seriousness.

Benjamin laughed, "I would have expected no less from you, mother."

"Good, I will tell your sister and Jean in the morning."

"When I speak with Hannah and her family tomorrow, I will let them know that you are staying, and she and her father and brother can come to your aid should you need anything at all, since Hamish is no longer with us."

"He was a very kind man, and I would not be here today without his intervention that day in the square and I have never forgotten it."

"Nor have I, things might have ended very differently had it not been for him."

"Benjamin, I want you to know how very proud I am of you, of the man you have become. Your father would be so proud of you as well. You have been a most loving and thoughtful son, a wonderful brother, and soon to be a husband and father. But most importantly, you have demonstrated your loyalty to the cause and your fellow soldiers. You have lived by your truth and the strength of your convictions. I love you, my son, and will pray for your safe return each and every day," I said as I kissed him on the cheek.

"Thank you, mother, those words will live on in my soul forever, and mean more to me than you could imagine," he said as he embraced me tightly.

Hannah accepted Benjamin's proposal and he gave her the ring I had worn these many, many years, the ring I was given by Simon when we married. We were able to have one dinner, Benjamin, Hannah, Amelia, Jean, and I before Benjamin left us. It was a wonderful evening although bittersweet for all and it was sprinkled with both laughter and tears. Amelia understood my reasons for staying, I think she always knew that I would, but it is a more difficult decision than I imagined it would be. There are only a few more days before she and Jean depart and then I will be here alone for the first time in my life, with no other member of my family in my home. Well truly, Fiona is like a sister to me now, and my brother and nieces and nephews are just a short ride away but still, it will be unnerving nonetheless.

The days pass quickly as we work to gather up all the things Amelia will take with her. Jean has arranged for a generous amount of space on the ship, and she is able to take with her the furniture from her room and some of the dishes and silver I had set aside for her trousseau. I am even sending with her the Italian glassware that had been a wedding gift from Simon's mother. I also carefully selected a few items of Simon's from his study to send with her, so that she will have a bit of her father always nearby. Lastly, I chose several of my best pieces of jewelry, some for her and some for the daughter I hoped this child she was carrying would be.

The night before she left, very much as Benjamin and I had done just a few days before, we had sat together on the couch in the study talking, reminiscing.

"Mother you have been very generous and thoughtful with your gifts, and I want you to know how very much I appreciate your kindness. I will be so happy to have a part of you with me every day," she said as she smiled at me.

"I wish I could have seen my way clear to go with you, but I hope you understand, my decision is not a reflection of my deep love and respect for you."

"I know mother, we understand, truly we do."

"Please know how very proud I am of you and how you have stood by Benjamin and Nathaniel, even during that time when you had to do so in secret. Just as they have done, you have been true to what you believe and have not been afraid to take action when others might have hesitated. You have been so strong and so courageous.

"Thank you mother, that is very kind of you, but you know, of course, that I have come by my nature because of you. I have wanted nothing more in my life than to emulate your strength, your loving nature, and your faithfulness to father, to this family, to me. It does my heart good to know that I have made you proud. But mother, know that my proudest moment in this life so far has been to call myself your daughter," she said as we embraced.

I held her tightly, suddenly feeling the weight of her departure settling down on my shoulders. I hated for her to go; I would like nothing more than to be with her when this child is born to help her in this new chapter of her life. But I also knew she did not need me. She might wish for me to be with her, but she did not need me to be, for she is the most confident and capable woman that I have ever known. Amelia is going to grow and prosper in her new life, of that I have no doubt and I need not worry for her future, of that I am certain.

"I love you Amelia, I will pray for your safe passage and your safe delivery. I ask only that you write when you can, I will be anxious to hear all your news."

"I will mother, I promise, I love you," she said smiling.

Chapter Fourteen

Finding the Way Home

It has been over a year since Amelia and Benjamin left and Fiona and I have fallen into a rhythm of our own. She stays full-time with me now as I often need help during the night and she sleeps in the room just next door, Benjamin's old room. I do not know what I would do without her, and she has become most precious to me.

"Mrs. Eliza, there is a letter here from Nathaniel," she said as she brought in the post.

I opened it and could barely believe what I was reading, he is on his way to Boston and should be here in the next few days. I have not seen him in many years since the siege ended and he returned to Pennsylvania. It will do my heart so much good to see him, but sadly, his wife and child are not coming. Nonetheless, it will be a joyous occasion.

"Fiona, we should get together a few things for a special dinner," I said.

"Indeed, I will see what I can find," she said gleefully.

The fighting has all been to the south these last few years with the French now playing a major role in the conflict by providing significant support and naval ships. There are times when I did not think we would prevail and challenges, like the defection of one General Benedict Arnold, have taken their toll but we have always rallied. I do not know what brings Nathaniel to Boston but no matter, whatever it may be I am just happy it has brought him here.

Fiona and I do our best to tidy the house and I was able to borrow some sugar from Elizabeth to make an apple tart. Necessaries continue to be in short supply from time to time but we have learned to make do, borrowing and trading with each other. I have sold all but one of the horses, and he is now kept in the barn of a friend so that Ethan is no longer needed. We have a cow, a dozen or so hens, and two roosters, and Fiona and I tend to a large garden every day to grow as much of our own food as we can. Richard has been generous in his support, and we can buy meat, cloth, oil, and yarn whenever it is available. We are not where we were before the war began but we do not want for the fundamentals of a decent life.

I was working in the kitchen with my back to the door when Nathaniel arrived.

"Mother, I never imagined you baking in this kitchen," said a male voice I barely recognized.

"Nathaniel!"

"Good afternoon mother, it is wonderful to see you," he said as we embraced.

He had aged, of course he had, we all have. He has a full beard, and his hair is graying at the temples, but he's wearing a fine suit and looking very distinguished.

"Son, you look well, but grayer than the last time I saw you."

Nathaniel laughed, "Yes that is true, and it is getting grayer every day I am afraid. Josiah and his sister are responsible for some of it, the British for the rest!"

"You have a daughter!" I exclaimed.

"Yes, we do, she was born about five months ago. Her name is Rebecca Sills Parkman, Sills being Emily's mother's surname before we married."

"That is wonderful Nathaniel."

"Benjamin sends his regards. I saw him about a month ago, he was headed to Charleston," said Nathaniel.

"What brings you to Boston? Since Emily and the children are not with you, I assume you are not here to stay?"

"You are correct, I am on my way to France with John Adams, we are boarding a ship here in just a few days."

"France, why are you going with Mr. Adams to France?" I asked with surprise.

"We are meeting with a British delegation there, believe it or not. Mother, we are starting discussions to bring about an end to this war," said Nathaniel with pride.

"My son, we have won. The war is over?"

"Almost, we hope by the time we sit down with them word will come from South Carolina that we have prevailed there. We have been beating them at every turn for the last few months and if General Green is the man we think he is, he will crush Colonel Tarleton and Lord Cornwallis."

I sat down at the small table in the kitchen and wiped my hands on my apron. It is almost over.

"Nathaniel, I am so very pleased by this news. You and your brother have made me proud beyond measure and I know your father would be proud too."

"Thank you, mother, but do not forget about Amelia. Without her help we might have lost the war before it even began," he said with a laugh. "What is the news of Amelia and Jean?"

"Has she not written you?"

"Perhaps she has but I have not received any-thing for some time."

"She also has a daughter. She is nearly a year old, and she is with child again. She and Jean have named the little girl Marie-Elizabeth Cusson Beauchamp. Quite a name for a little girl," I said smiling.

We spent the rest of the evening talking about the war, our family, and enjoying each other's company. I was grateful for these few days with him. But as I was preparing for bed, I was also thinking that Nathaniel's sudden appearance here and his trip to France might offer me an opportunity that I did not think I would have. I shall speak to him in the morning.

"Nathaniel, do you think I might be able to accompany you to France?" I asked as we sat down to breakfast.

"Mother, you want to go to France?"

"I do, while I am glad that I stayed here when Amelia and Jean left, I have been wishing I had gone with her and thought there would be no way to remedy that mistake. But perhaps now there is."

"If that is what you wish I can certainly see if there is room on the ship but, mother, I do not know when you would be able to return."

"I do not intend to return; Fiona can manage until Benjamin comes home."

"I see," he said thoughtfully. "Are you sure, mother?"

"Yes, I am. I have never been more sure of anything in my life."

Nathaniel was able to secure space for me and we will be leaving the day after tomorrow. This time I packed only one trunk, clothes mostly, and a few things I wanted Amelia to pass on to her children. Everything else could stay for Benjamin and Nathaniel to share among themselves and their children. I had only to say goodbye to Fiona and I would be on my way.

"Mrs. Eliza, I do not know why you want to do this now, but if that is your wish I pray only for your safe passage and your continued health," she said.

"Fiona, I have come to understand that while this is indeed my home, my heart is scattered across the world with my children and my husband. As I come closer to the end of my life, I realize being with them is more important to me than being on this soil, in this place."

"I understand," she replied as a single tear made its way down her face.

"You have been as a sister to me these last years, and your loyalty and care have meant more to me, Fiona, than I could ever repay. Benjamin will be happy to see that you are still here for him and his family, and they are very lucky to have you," I said as we embraced.

"I promise you I will do my best to care for Master Benjamin and his family."

"I know you will Fiona, thank you, for everything.

"Goodbye Eliza," she replied before excusing herself, not wanting to shed her tears in front of me.

I watched Boston from the railing of the ship as we sailed out of the harbor and a peacefulness came over me that I had not felt in some time. Nathaniel stood with me as we watched the landscape fade from view. We would be in France in about two months' time or so depending on the winds and I would relish this time spent with him. I also found John Adams to be a brilliant and well-spoken man and the three of us spent much time together talking about their plans for the new government. I could see the respect that Mr. Adams had for Nathaniel, and I was very pleased by that.

There had been no time to get a letter to Amelia to let her know I was coming so it was agreed that I would stay with Nathaniel until word could be sent to her. I hope that it will be received well and that this surprise will not be an unpleasant one. Simon intended to take me to Paris one day, but we never did make the trip, so I am looking forward to seeing a bit of the city before I join Amelia and Jean in Chartres, the small town of his birth. The sailing was uneventful, and we arrived in just nine weeks' time which they say is quite good. I am glad to be off the ship finally and surprised that the bustling wharf in Paris is much larger than the one in Boston. The air is filled with the sounds of many more languages and accents and styles of clothing than I had imagined.

The carriage ride to the home of the friend of John Adams where we will be staying was unexpected and exposed Paris for what it really was. Despite the beautiful buildings and fountains, the city was dark and dirty. The streets were overcrowded, and young filthy children begged or stole at every corner. A sense of despair and hopelessness hung over the city like a thick cloud of smoke lingers from a fire. I have quickly changed my mind about seeing any of the city, but instead will wait patiently until I can make my way to Amelia.

It was nearly a week before Jean arrived to take me to their home.

"Madame Parkman, Je ne m'attendais pas à avoir
à nouveau le plaisir de votre compagnie, mais je suis
très heureux de vous voir."

"In English, Jean," I said with a smile.

"Yes, oh yes I have forgotten, I never expected to
have the pleasure of your company again, but I am
most happy to see you!"

"Thank you, Jean, I am very happy to see you
too. I am grateful to you for coming. I hope my arrival
is not unwelcome," I said at last.

"Of course not, Amelia can hardly wait to see
you and, of course, she is anxious for you to meet our
petit précieux, our little precious one. As she is with
child again, I thought the carriage ride, which can be
quite bumpy, might best be avoided, but she is most
anxious so we should be on our way."

"Jean, before we go, this is my son Nathaniel, I
do not believe you two had an opportunity to meet
when you were in the Colonies."

"C'est avec grand plaisir que je rencontre votre
Monsieur Beauchamp," Nathaniel said with a slight
bow.

"Ah, another Parkman with impeccable French I see!" said Jean as he shook hands with Nathaniel. "Now we must go Madame so that we will be out of the city before dark."

"Indeed, thank you Nathaniel, for helping me get this far, and I wish you and Mr. Adams success with your negotiations. You will come to see us when you have an opportunity?"

"Oui s'il vous plaît faire, Nathaniel."

"Thank you for the invitation, Jean, I would very much like to come and see my sister and meet my niece," he said with a slight bow.

"Now, mother, I must be going," he said as he kissed me on both cheeks.

"Au revoir," I said with a smile.

The distance we needed to travel was not long, but the carriage was slow getting out of the city as we had to pick our way carefully among the crowd. Beggars frequently hammered on the windows asking for money and it was an unsettling, if not frightening, experience. Jean and I talked the entire trip which helped to keep my mind off our surroundings, and once out of the city it was beautiful to behold.

"We have also a surprise for you," said Jean as the carriage pulled up in front of a beautiful chateau. "It was not planned but eh, it is here nonetheless," he said smiling.

I could not imagine what it might be, something to do with Amelia or perhaps Marie-Elizabeth I did not know, but I was beyond excited to see Amelia and a woman holding a small child waiting out front when we stopped.

"There she is, Elizabeth, your Grand-mère has arrived," said Amelia, taking the child into her arms.

"Mother, it is so good to see you," said Amelia. "This is your granddaughter, Marie-Elizabeth, but we call her Eliza for short," she said smiling.

"Good day, you darling child," I said as I took her in my arms. She stared at me the way babies do when they are surprised and delighted at the same time. She looked very much like Amelia as a young child except for her head of dark hair which she got from her father.

I embraced Amelia the best I could, but she was quite heavy with child, and seeing her I am glad that Jean made her stay behind. There were introductions all around as we made our way into the house.

"Mother, there is one more person I would like to introduce.

Actually, he may not need an introduction at all, but it has been some time," she said slyly.

There, standing by the stairs, was a gentleman the spitting image of Simon when he was a younger man. At first, I thought perhaps it was a relative of his, but then when the man smiled, I knew at once who it was.

"Richard, oh my goodness, Richard, what are you doing here!"

"I came to see you, of course!" he said as we embraced.

I held him tightly, hardly believing he was here. I truly thought I would never see him again and yet here he was in France of all places.

"But you cannot be here to see me, you did not know I was coming!" I said with confusion.

"I jest with you, mother; I am here in France on business, and I came to see Amelia and to meet my niece. I did not know you would be here until word came from Nathaniel, but I am most pleased to see you," he said with a voice that seems to have gotten deeper with age.

"Oh, Richard, I am so glad, and Nathaniel will be coming too when he can, and we can all, well almost all of us, be together. It is wonderful indeed."

The afternoon and into the late hour of the evening was spent deep in conversation with Amelia and Richard catching up on all that has transpired since I had seen them last. Amelia has only one more month till her confinement, and she is looking healthy and happy. Eliza is a joy and an easy baby she says, and she is very much looking forward to the birth of this child, with a plan to fill the nursery with several more.

Richard has not married again. Instead, he spends his time on business making sure things are running smoothly and trying to make sure things are profitable. While he is happy in Barbados, he is ready to go home, and he has been working with a man he now trusts enough to leave him in charge there. His plan is to return to Boston as soon as the war is over, which sounds like it might be soon. We will know more when Nathaniel comes.

The next few weeks pass quickly, and we enjoy our days together playing with Eliza, and it feels like we are a family again for the first time in a long time. I miss John. I wish things had not ended with him so badly. If he were still with us maybe there would have been a chance of reconciliation, but that chance has been snatched away by the grim reaper who once again has sought payment from one of my sons. But it is not John who I miss the most. It is Simon. More and more, I have felt the loss of my dearest husband. My life has not felt complete since his passing, a void which I have not been able to fill, and still a guilt about not going with him to England.

Nathaniel has written to say he will join us tomorrow and Richard will also return from his trip to visit a buyer so we will all be together again, at least for a day or two. This is good because there are some words that need to be spoken and it is best I do it when we are all together. A letter has been sent to Benjamin and to Fiona regarding my plans and so soon all will be known. I sleep restlessly, anxious for the morning to come and as I am up before the others, I make my way to the nursery and find Marie-Elizabeth sitting in her bassinette.

"Good morning, my love, you are up very early this fine day."

She smiles and coos and we talk about her grandfather, her uncles Benjamin and John, and Boston. I tell her how lucky she is to have such a wonderful mother and father and how the world is all ahead of her just as mine is all behind me. Every day, the change becomes more profound. It is hard to catch my breath, and there is little I can do without frequent rest. No longer can I walk without my cane and when I stand next to my children, I realize how much smaller in stature I have become. I am wasting away a bit every moment of every day. It is almost time, and I am ready. There is just one thing left to do.

Dinner is a lovely affair. Amelia has dressed the table with the china and glasses I had sent with her, and it is resplendent. Everyone is dressed in their finest, Amelia has even lent me one of her older gowns as I had brought nothing with me to match the magnificence of the evening.

I cleared my throat, "My heart is very full at this moment, to see you all here, so happy and so well and we should drink a toast to your father, and John, and send our best wishes to Benjamin," I said as I raised my glass.

"To father," said Nathaniel.

"To John," said Richard.

"For Benjamin," said Amelia.

"I suppose you are all wondering why I changed my mind and decided to come to France after all, but in fact I did not, I am not staying in France."

"What do you mean mother, you are not staying?" asked Amelia, alarmed.

"No, I never intended to stay. I came to see you, to meet Marie-Elizabeth, to spend some time with Nathaniel and, unexpectedly but most happily, with Richard. But I am going to England. As soon as I arrived in Paris, I made arrangements to travel on a Dutch ship to London and I leave in just a few days."

"Mother, I do not understand," said Richard.

"I do," said Nathaniel as he smiled at me.

"Ah, I thought you might Nathaniel, you are so much like your father, and you know me quite well.

I thought I would never leave Boston. It was my home and the land there my birthright. Even Simon thought that I would never leave, that I should not leave. But he was wrong. Home is not a place of brick and mortar or the dirt upon which what you build sits. It is the place where the love and joy of family and those you care most about resides. It is the place you feel safe and loved and for me that place is no longer truly in Boston. My loves, you are scattered to the wind in all corners of the globe. But as I come to the end of my life, the place where I feel most safe and most loved is with your father. I should have stayed with him; he never should have gone on to England alone. But now, I will make it right."

"Mother, you never read the letter that father left for Benjamin and me before he left for England but trust me when I say he never felt abandoned by you. He knew you would go with him to the ends of the earth if need be, without question or hesitation, as he knew your love for him was true and constant. You should feel no guilt, mother, no remorse, but I for one endorse your desire to be buried next to father and it will give me peace knowing that you two are together."

"Mother, I agree with Nathaniel but how will you manage in London alone?" asked Amelia.

"I will not be alone. I have been in contact with William and he and his wife, Catherine, have invited me to stay with them on the grounds of the Parkman Estate. I did not want to intrude on Simon's nephew, David, but he was happy to support my stay with William and I graciously accepted."

"It seems as if it is settled then, I will return you to Paris when I go the day after tomorrow and you may stay with me until your ship departs," said Nathaniel.

"We have each said our goodbyes before and so I feel we need not say them again, so let us not be sorrowful but happy to have spent this time together. My love for you, each of you, has never faltered and my wish for you and for your children, and all your descendants who follow is that you each find home, the place where you are safe and loved."

"To Madame Parkman," said Jean as he raised his glass.

"To mother," they all chimed in.

The sailing was short and without trouble and I was relieved to see William standing on the dock waiting for me. I assumed the woman with him was his wife, Catherine. They had married last year, and both are in service at the Parkman Estate for which I am most grateful. A young man carried my small bag and held my arm down the gangplank, and I held tightly to my cane in my other hand. The solid ground was a welcome respite from the movement of the ship. The trip was not long but the seas had been very rough, and I was grateful we had arrived.

"Mrs. Parkman," called out William, waving his arms so I could better find him in the crowd.

"William, I am so happy to see you," I said, as he embraced me more tightly than I would have expected.

"Mrs. Parkman, may I introduce my wife, Catherine," he said, gesturing to the small woman standing behind him.

"Mrs. Parkman, it is my pleasure to meet you. William has told me so much about you and your family."

"The pleasure is mine, Catherine, I am beyond grateful that you and William have opened your home to me," I said, taking her hand in mine.

"It is our honor Mrs. Parkman, truly," she said as she squeezed my hand.

"Let us get you home. You must be very tired," said William.

"William, would you mind if we stopped at the cemetery before we go to the house?"

His eyes softened, "No Ma'am, I do not mind. It is on the way."

Catherine and I rode along in companionable silence as William drove through the streets of London. I had not been here in many years, and it has grown beyond my wildest imagining. As I looked upon the throngs of people doing their marketing, talking, and laughing with one another, it strikes me that this has been, for the last ten years, our enemy. We have been killing them and they us. I shook my head and the thought that has plagued me since Simon William died fills my thoughts again. Why can man not find a way to resolve their differences without resorting to death and destruction. We are intelligent creatures, yet we cannot seem to escape our baser instincts as if we were shoeless creatures of the forest.

As we left the crowded streets, the world opened to green pastures, forests, and the cobblestones gave way to a dusty dirt road. After a time, I could see the estate come into view. It was as picturesque as I remembered. Simon brought me here to meet his parents right after we wed. It had impressed me immensely then, and it is no less impressive now. As we came through the stone archway, I could still make out the word Parkman engraved on the stone as it had been for hundreds of years. The grounds were impeccably kept, and all the flowers were in bloom. It was a beautiful sight indeed.

We veered off the main road before reaching the house and there, tucked in among the trees, was the Parkman family cemetery. A large crypt occupied the center with rows of large obelisks and headstones surrounding it. A wrought iron fence enclosed the entire property, and, like the grounds, it was immaculately maintained, not so much as a blade of grass was out of place. There were many large trees and the sun filtered through the leaves in rays of gold which sparkled with the gentle breeze. William stopped outside the gate.

"This is as close as I can get in the carriage, Mrs. Parkman," he said as he climbed down to help me out. "Master Parkman is buried just over here," he said as he pointed out a beautiful gray stone obelisk just to our right.

"Would you like me to walk with you?" asked Catherine.

"No thank you, my dear, not this time, I would like to go alone if I may."

"Of course, I understand, we are in no hurry, take as much time as you need. Master David has given us the whole day off to get you settled."

"Thank you, I will have to remember to thank him."

I walked slowly across the grass until I was standing in front of the obelisk carved with Simon's name, his date of birth, and death. I traced the letters with my fingers, feeling the ridges of each one in turn. It was a beautiful monument and there was ample room for a name below. It glinted in the sun with a richness that warmed my soul. I do not know who had chosen this, but I was most pleased by it. It was David no doubt, one more thing to thank him for. I looked around this place, reading the names of the family members who surround Simon in his eternal rest. There were many of them with most of their names unfamiliar to me. The large crypt contained the remains of his great-grandparents, grandparents, and parents.

A rustling in a nearby tree caught my attention but I did not see anything at first. I watched the tree for a moment to see if anything should appear and after a moment a bird emerged. It was a red-tailed hawk that flew out of the tree and climbed toward the sky, circling slowly overhead before flying off toward the house. I leaned my cheek against the cool hard stone, and put my hands on the name carved there, "I am here, Simon, I am home," I whispered.